RAVES REVIEWS FOR A. R. GURNEY

LATER LIFE

"Extremely funny and very touching."   —HOWARD KISSEL, *Daily News*

"Charmingly clever . . . immeasurably touching."   —*New York Post*

"*Later Life* offers one of our best playwrights at the top of his form."
—*Variety*

THE SNOW BALL

"Pure enchantment of a nostalgic, humorous and uplifting nature about life among affluent New England WASPs."   —*San Diego Times*

"A fabulous journey, blending the glamour of ballroom dancing with one man's yearning for the glorious days of yesteryear."
—*Register Citizen* (Connecticut)

THE OLD BOY

"Entertaining . . . The climactic battle is as powerful as anything this playwright has written."   —FRANK RICH, *New York Times*

"Surprising and profound. A compelling work!"   —*Daily News*

"A polished gem of humor and pathos. Beautifully structured!" —*Variety*

A. R. GURNEY, winner of the 1987 Award of Merit from the American Academy and Institute of Arts and Letters, has written over seventeen plays, among them *The Cocktail Hour, Love Letters, The Dining Room, Another Antigone, Scenes from American Life, Children, Richard Cory, The Wayside Motor Inn, The Middle Ages, What I Did Last Summer, The Golden Age, Sweet Sue,* and *The Fourth Wall.* He is also the author of three novels: *The Snow Ball, The Gospel According to Joe,* and *Entertaining Strangers.* Gurney won a Drama Desk Award in 1971, a Rockefeller Award in 1977, a National Endowment Award in 1982 and a Lucille Lortel Award in 1989. He is also a member of the Artistic Board of Playwrights Horizons in New York City, where many of his works have been performed.

A. R. GURNEY

LATER LIFE

AND TWO OTHER PLAYS:
THE SNOW BALL AND THE OLD BOY

A PLUME BOOK

PLUME

Published by the Penguin Group
Penguin Books USA Inc., 375 Hudson Street, New York, New York 10014, U.S.A.
Penguin Books Ltd, 27 Wrights Lane, London W8 5TZ, England
Penguin Books Australia Ltd, Ringwood, Victoria, Australia
Penguin Books Canada Ltd, 10 Alcorn Avenue, Toronto, Ontario, Canada M4V 3B2
Penguin Books (N.Z.) Ltd, 182–190 Wairau Road, Auckland 10, New Zealand

Penguin Books Ltd, Registered Offices:
Harmondsworth, Middlesex, England

This volume published by Plume, an imprint of Dutton Signet,
a division of Penguin Books USA Inc.

First Printing, May, 1994
1 3 5 7 9 10 8 6 4 2

OLD GLOBE THEATRE HARTFORD STAGE COMPANY
San Diego, California Hartford, Connecticut

Artistic Director Artistic Director
Jack O'Brien Mark Lamos

Managing Director Managing Director
Thomas Hall David Hawkanson

SPECIAL NOTE ON SONGS AND MUSIC
For performance of such songs and music mentioned in this play as are in copyright, the permission of the copyright owners must be obtained; or other songs and music in the public domain substituted.

Ⓟ REGISTERED TRADEMARK—MARCA REGISTRADA

LIBRARY OF CONGRESS CATALOGING-IN-PUBLICATION DATA
Gurney, A. R. (Albert Ramsdell).
Later life : and two other plays, The snow ball and The old boy /
A.R. Gurney.
p. cm.
ISBN 0-452-27251-3
1. WASPS (Persons)—New England—Drama. 2. Middle aged persons—
New England—Drama. I. Title.
PS3557.U82L37 1994
812'.54—dc20   93-48843
CIP

Printed in the United States of America
Set in Bembo

Designed by Steven N. Stathakis

BOOKS ARE AVAILABLE AT QUANTITY DISCOUNTS WHEN USED TO PROMOTE PRODUCTS OR SERVICES. FOR INFORMATION PLEASE WRITE TO PREMIUM MARKETING DIVISION, PENGUIN BOOKS USA INC., 375 HUDSON STREET, NEW YORK, NEW YORK 10014.

INTRODUCTION

Over the years, I've come to think of my plays somewhat as I do my own children—specific entities I've helped create and educate, but who finally are free to seek their own fortune. Here I'm introducing my three latest offspring, all recently graduated from initial productions and now out to stake some claim for themselves in the larger world.

In appearance, these three "children" seem to come from the same family. They all have to do with middle-aged men attempting to make some accommodation with their pasts. I would hope, however, that they are also different enough to make their own separate impressions. Certainly, they are different in form and shape. *The Snow Ball*, the oldest of the three, is an elaborate quasi-musical, calling for a large cast and complex visual effects. *The Old Boy* looks trim and Spartan, but tells a rather complicated and involuted story. *Later Life*, the most recent of the three, is the shortest and simplest on the surface, but perhaps has the most intricate subtext.

Parents can become biased and boring when they talk about their own children, who usually are best left to speak for themselves. Nonetheless, I'll try to talk about these plays with some sort of detachment, and to give some suggestion of their background and upbringing.

The Snow Ball was originally a novel, published by Arbor House in 1984. You can still find it in paperback in a few bookstores. I had initially envisioned it as a play, but as I wrote it, I felt that it would cost too much to produce, so it became a book. In 1990, my friend Jack O'Brien, who had directed my play *The Cocktail Hour* with such enthusiasm and humor, suggested I try "working with a larger palette." He had read my novel and liked it, so I proposed that I try to return it to the stage by writing it as a new play with old music.

The process of transition proved much more difficult than I had expected. Cooper Jones, who was comfortable as the narrator in the book, became less so on stage. I had to drag him into the light and persuade him to be more actively dramatic. Conversely, Jack and Kitty, the romantic couple Cooper is obsessed with, didn't want to get off. They kept threatening to take over the main plot, and perhaps one could argue that they succeeded. In any case, with O'Brien as director, Graciela Daniele as choreographer, Douglas Schmidt as designer, and a fine cast of accommodating actors, we went into rehearsal and managed to slap the play into some sort of shape during a series of tryout productions at the Hartford Stage Company, the Old Globe Theatre in San Diego, and finally the Huntington Theatre in Boston.

The Snow Ball is about the lures and dangers of nostalgia, as Cooper Jones gets sucked into the idea of reviving a legendary party and bringing back the couple who had once danced so well at it. Ballroom dancing becomes, for him, an image for idealized male-female behavior, very different from the contemporary pushes and pulls which characterize his own marriage. But snow melts, and the past fades, and Jack and Kitty have gotten older; so at the end Cooper has finally learned to face a less sentimental future on a new footing with his no-nonsense wife, Liz.

The Snow Ball, as a play, melted away, too. It seemed to please enough audiences along the way to Boston that several producers were interested in taking it farther. A contemptuous review in the *Boston Globe*, however, frightened them off fast. It's hard to blame them. It's a risky play, with a large cast and complicated sets and costumes. It looks and feels like a musical, yet nobody sings in it—everybody is too busy trying to dance. In any case, the play never came to New York, which for better or worse is the ultimate imprimatur of theatrical success in our country, and Jack Daley and Kitty Price are now back dancing on the printed page, rather than on the stage I thought they were destined for.

The Old Boy, on the other hand, was born in the heart of New York, at Playwrights Horizons, where several other plays of mine have also had their start. It was directed with great energy and style by John Rubinstein, and received reviews that were qualified enough to intimidate another group of producers who had shown interest in it during previews. The play wasn't helped much, either, when its excellent cast was suddenly decimated by lucrative offers from a television miniseries. Off they went to Hollywood on short notice. We didn't have enough understudies to replace them, so the play collapsed almost before it had a chance to walk. Since then, with some rewriting, it has staggered back onto its feet in several other commendable productions, and has been bought by Hollywood, so that possibly it will find a life for itself after all.

As in *The Snow Ball*, the protagonist of *The Old Boy* is drawn into the past. Here, though, the motivation is not simply sentimental or nostalgic; there is a dissonance in his heart that needs to be resolved. Sam has an almost instinctive need, like the Atlantic salmon, to return to the source of his anxiety—in this case, a prestigious New England boarding school where he spent his formative years. There he discovers how he once seriously affected several other lives and, by a kind of public self-examination and confession, does what he can to right those wrongs and thereby soothe the ache in his own soul.

The subject of *The Old Boy* is not really homosexuality. The play, rather, makes use of that particular issue to dramatize the dangers of conformity, and the price we all pay when we force ourselves and others into conventional patterns of behavior. I like to think there are some vivid, actable characters here, and some strong scenes, but there is also a problematic climax which

I never quite got right. I'm beginning to wonder whether Sam's confessional speech is, in itself, a theatrical convention which doesn't belong in a play so focused on challenging conventional modes. Yet I never could find a better way of doing it. Perhaps the film medium, in its ability to cut from a speech to those on whom it is having an effect, will resolve this problem, if it is one. Another issue in the play may be its milieu. Like *The Snow Ball*, its setting may simply be too parochial for general appeal. Wasps at boarding school, as at dancing school, hardly pulse with contemporary resonance. Still, I'm proud of this play and what it tries to say and do.

In *Later Life*, the past steps up and shakes Austin by the hand. Set in Boston, a city rich with American tradition, the play dramatizes the pressures of the past by watching them seep into the present. There are no flashbacks here, yet all the characters bring on stage with them a considerable amount of ancient history. And they all, including the city itself, are attempting to shake off the cobwebs and move forward in one way or another.

Except for Austin, the protagonist. For the second time in his life, he is given a chance to take a new step, by reaching out to Ruth. Once again he is unable to. His proposal to her is ultimately civilized, but also ultimately lifeless. At the end of the play, he stands like a ghost, outside the human community, clutching a forgotten sweater.

The play really asks the question whether in later life, we are simply exaggerations and extensions of our earlier selves, or whether we can change and grow as we grow older. Austin and Ruth would seem to embody the former position, though Ruth instinctively chooses a turbulent life over what bodes to be a kind of genteel death. The other characters are examples of human resiliency and changeability, dramatized by the fact that two actors are asked to play so many different roles. Boston itself, in its ability to adapt and respond to the times, is also living out its own later life.

As I was writing this play, I realized that Austin's sense of his own personal doom was similar to that of Henry James's tormented hero in his novella *The Beast in the Jungle,* which I had taught several times in my own earlier life at M.I.T. In this sense, my play is an adaptation of James's story, but I would argue that in its form and setting it is very different. Jamesian or not, I find Austin's predicament infinitely sad—a man encumbered by so much baggage from the past that he is unable to seize life, even when it presents itself to him in such an enticing way.

Later Life, like *The Old Boy,* opened at Playwrights Horizons in New York; it was directed by the new artistic director, Don Scardino. As I write this, the play is in the process of transferring to the Westside Theatre for what we hope will be a long run. From its inception, this particular work seemed blessed, even if its hero is damned. The rehearsals were a joy, the cast delightfully imaginative, the audiences helpful during previews, and the critics mostly enthusiastic. Of all my children, this one had the easiest birth, and so far has been the easiest to bring up. Whether that means it will succeed better than its siblings in the long run remains to be seen. I have to say I have a special affection for it, since it so particularly embodies the collaborative pleasures of this strange, enticing profession we call theatre.

LATER LIFE

To Charles Kimbrough

Later Life was first produced at Playwrights Horizons (Don Scardino, artistic director) in New York City on May 23, 1993. It was directed by Don Scardino; the set was by Ben Edwards; the costumes were by Jennifer Von Mayrhauser; the lighting was by Brian MacDevitt; the sound was by Guy Sherman; the wigs were by Daniel Platten; and the production stage manager was Dianne Trulock. The cast was as follows:

AUSTIN   *Charles Kimbrough*
RUTH   *Maureen Anderman*
OTHER MEN   *Anthony Heald*
OTHER WOMEN   *Carole Shelley*

The play moved to the Westside Theatre, where it reopened on August 10, 1993. It was produced there by Stephen Baruch, Richard Frankel, and Thomas Viertel, along with the Shubert Organization. At this theatre, the part of Austin was played by Edmond Genest, followed by Josef Sommer.

CHARACTERS

AUSTIN

RUTH

SALLY
MARION
NANCY   } to be played by one actress
ESTHER
JUDITH

JIM
ROY
DUANE   } to be played by one actor
TED
WALT

SETTING

The terrace off an apartment in a high-rise building overlooking Boston Harbor. Good outdoor furniture, including a chaise. A hurricane candle and an ashtray on an upstage table. Occasional greenery. Several chrysanthemum plants to suggest the fall. A romantic, starry sky behind.

The play is to be performed without an intermission.

The author is indebted to Henry James.

Before rise:

Elegant music such as Scarlatti or Vivaldi.

At rise:

Evening light, early September.

The music is now heard coming from within, along with sounds of a lively party. The stage is empty. We hear occasional harbor sounds—a buoy bell, a foghorn.

SALLY *comes on, busily. She wears whatever a hostess would wear.*

SALLY (*beckoning toward within*): Come out here, Austin! (*She adjusts a couple of chairs so that they face more toward each other. She speaks more to herself.*) I'm setting the stage here. That's all I can do. Just set the stage. . . . (*Again toward within:*) I said, come on out.

(AUSTIN *comes out, somewhat hesitantly. He is a distinguished, good-looking, middle-aged man, who wears a gray suit, a blue shirt, and a conservative tie. He carries a glass.*)

Now wait here.

AUSTIN: Why should I wait here?

SALLY: So you can talk.

AUSTIN: To you?

SALLY: No, not to me, Austin. I'm much too busy to talk. (*She lights the outdoor candle.*) I want you to talk to *her.*

AUSTIN: Who's "her"?

SALLY: You'll see.

AUSTIN: Oh, Sally . . .

SALLY: No, Austin, it's time you took a chance. I'll go get her. (*She starts back in.*) Now please. Just wait.

AUSTIN (*calling after her*): What do I do while I wait?

SALLY (*adjusting his tie*): You think. You admire the view of Boston Harbor. You examine your immortal soul. I don't care, as long as you wait.

> (*She hurries off.*)
> (AUSTIN *waits, uneasily.*)
> (JIM *comes out. He might wear a beard or a mustache, and is rather scruffily dressed.*)

JIM: I believe this is where people may still smoke.

AUSTIN: I should think so. Yes.

JIM (*going to the ashtray on the table*): That looks very much like an ashtray.

AUSTIN: I guess it is.

JIM (*examining it*): It is indeed. It is definitely an ashtray. (*Holding it up:*) Appealing object, isn't it? Notice the shape.

AUSTIN: Yes.

JIM: Do you suppose there are still people in the world who design ashtrays?

AUSTIN: I imagine there are. . . . In Europe.

JIM (*producing an unopened pack of Marlboros*): Speaking of design, this pack itself also has a subtle appeal. Notice the brightness of the red, the crispness of the lettering, the abstract white mountain peak behind, luring us on.

AUSTIN: Oh, yes. I see.

JIM: Do you realize that at least eighty percent of the price we pay for cigarettes goes for packaging and taxes?

AUSTIN: I didn't know that.

JIM: And with Clinton in, the tax will be substantially higher.

AUSTIN: Yes, well, Clinton . . .

JIM (*opening the pack carefully*): On the other hand, the packaging is important. There is nothing sweeter than the smell of fresh tobacco. (*He holds it out to* AUSTIN.) Smell.

AUSTIN: Oh, well . . .

JIM: No, I'm serious. Smell.

(AUSTIN *takes the pack and sniffs.*)

You see?

AUSTIN (*handing it back*): It's quite pleasant. . . .

JIM: Pleasant? That is the aroma of rural America. There is a hint of the Virginia planter in that, and the stolid yeomen farmers of the North Carolina plains, coupled with the personal cologne of Senator Jesse Helms.

AUSTIN: Ha ha.

JIM (*beginning to tap out a cigarette*): This is also a pleasant process. Tapping the first one out. Gently coaxing him away from his companions. All the time knowing that there are nineteen others, waiting patiently for their turn. . . . Oh. Excuse me. Want one? (*He offers* AUSTIN *one.*)

AUSTIN: No thanks.

JIM: Sure?

AUSTIN: Positive.

JIM: You don't smoke?

AUSTIN: No.

JIM: Never did?

AUSTIN: No.

JIM: Not even when everyone else did?

AUSTIN: No.

JIM: Never even tried it?

AUSTIN: Oh, well, I suppose behind the barn. . . .

JIM (*taking a cigarette for himself*): That's too bad. You've missed
something in life. Smoking is one of the great pleasures of the
phenomenal world. It's the closest we come to heaven on
earth—particularly now it's forbidden fruit. (*He takes out a
lighter.*) It adds depth and dimension to whatever we say or
do. Oh, I know, I know: it corrupts children, it exploits the
Third World, it is gross, addictive, and unnecessary. It is an
image of capitalism in its last, most self-destructive stages. But
. . . (*He puts the cigarette in his mouth, lights the lighter, holds it
almost to his cigarette.*) It is also a gesture of freedom in an absurd
universe. (*He suddenly snaps the lighter shut.*) And I'm giving it
up.

AUSTIN: Are you serious?

JIM: I am. I have made the decision. That's why I'm behaving
like such an asshole.

AUSTIN: Oh, I wouldn't say that.

JIM: No, really. I've given it up before, of course, but tonight is
the big night. I bought this fresh pack, and came out here

because this time I'm trying to confront temptation. I am shaking hands with the devil. I am deliberately immersing myself in the dangerous element.

AUSTIN: Do you teach around here?

JIM: That's not important. What I do—or rather, what I did—was smoke. I was an existential smoker. I smoked, therefore I was.

AUSTIN: I'm sure you teach.

JIM: No, I smoked. I am what they call a recovering nicoholic. Or what *I* call tobacco-challenged. My days were comforted by this pleasant haze. My nights were highlighted by this glowing ash. Cigarettes provided the only significant punctuation in the sprawling, ungrammatical sentences which composed my life. And therefore, even though I was an outcast, a pariah, a scapegoat, I wore my badge of shame with honor. I flaunted it. Hey, it was my scarlet letter. (*He returns the cigarette to the pack.*)

AUSTIN (*laughing*): Come on. Where do you teach? Harvard? B.U.? M.I.T.? Where?

JIM: All right. I confess. I have taught. Philosophy. At Brandeis. They made me take early retirement last year. They claimed I slept with too many students.

AUSTIN: Oh, now . . .

JIM: But I think the real reason was I smoked.

AUSTIN: All right now. Enough's enough.

JIM: I agree. You must forgive me. (*Caressing the pack of cigarettes:*) But you see, I'm saying goodbye to a lifelong companion. Nothing becomes it like the leaving thereof. (*He sniffs it longingly.*) Yet it's an agonizing decision! All decisions are, at our age. For us, there's no turning back. Younger people can change their minds, change their lives, that's fine, they have a lifetime ahead of them to change again. But for us who have had a whiff of the grave—it all boils down to our last chance.

(SALLY *comes back out, with* RUTH *in tow.* RUTH *is a lovely woman, who wears a simple, slightly artsy dress. She carries a glass of white wine.*)

SALLY: Here we are! . . . Now go away, Jimmy. (*To* AUSTIN:) Has he been boring you about smoking?

JIM: I've given it up, Sal.

SALLY: So you said last week.

JIM: This time I am.

SALLY: Then go away and *do* it, Jimmy. I want these two people to talk.

JIM (*to* AUSTIN, *as he leaves*): Next time you see me, I'll be a shadow of my former self. I'll be a negative entity, defined not by what I am but by what I am not. You will perceive and know me simply as a Nonsmoker.

SALLY: Just go, Jimmy. Please.

JIM: All right. But I hope you'll remember me for when I came . . . and saw . . . and conquered the habit.

(JIM *goes. The party sounds continue within.*)

SALLY: He's a nice man, but he smokes.

AUSTIN: Give him a chance, Sally.

SALLY: I'm giving *you* a chance, Austin. . . . This is Ruth. . . .
And Ruth, this is Austin. . . .

AUSTIN (*extending his hand*): How do you do.

RUTH: Hello.

(*They shake hands.*)

SALLY: Ruth's from out of town.

AUSTIN: Then welcome to Boston.

SALLY (*looking from one to the other*): And?

RUTH: He doesn't remember.

SALLY (*to* AUSTIN): You don't remember Ruth?

AUSTIN: Should I?

SALLY: She remembers you.

RUTH: I do. I definitely do.

SALLY: She said she noticed you the minute you walked into
the room.

RUTH: Oh, not the *minute* . . .

SALLY (*to* AUSTIN): Did you notice *her*?

AUSTIN (*with a polite bow*): I certainly do now.

RUTH: I told you he wouldn't remember.

SALLY: Well, then *get* him to.

RUTH: I'll try.

SALLY: And let me break the ice here: Austin, I told Ruth you
were divorced, and I'm hereby telling you that Ruth is.

RUTH: Not divorced. Separated.

SALLY (*coming down to* RUTH): Judith said you were divorced.

RUTH: Judith thinks I should be.

SALLY (*recovering her equanimity*): Well, the point is, here you are. Now make the most of it.

(*She goes.*)
(*Pause.*)

AUSTIN: We've met?

RUTH: We have.

AUSTIN: When?

RUTH: Think back.

AUSTIN: To when?

RUTH: Just think.

AUSTIN: I'm thinking. . . . (*He looks at her carefully.*) Ruth, eh?

RUTH: Ruth.

AUSTIN: What's your last name?

RUTH: That won't help.

AUSTIN: What was your last name when we met?

RUTH: You never knew my last name.

AUSTIN: I just knew Ruth.

RUTH: That's all you knew.

(*Pause.*)

AUSTIN: Were you married?

RUTH: Then?

AUSTIN: When we met.

RUTH: Oh, no.

AUSTIN: Was I?

RUTH: No.

AUSTIN: Ah. Then we're talking about way back.

RUTH: Way, way back.

AUSTIN: Were we in college?

RUTH: No.

AUSTIN: School, then.

RUTH: I doubt if we would have met either at school or at college.

AUSTIN: Why not?

RUTH: Not everybody in the world went to Groton and Harvard.

AUSTIN: So I have learned in the course of my life. . . .

(RUTH *laughs*.)

I feel like a fool.

RUTH: Why?

AUSTIN: An attractive woman came into my life. And I don't remember.

RUTH: My hair was different then.

AUSTIN: Still. This is embarrassing.

RUTH: You want a hint?

AUSTIN: No, I should get it on my own. . . . (*He looks at her carefully.*) There's something. . . . Goddammit, I pride myself on my memory! I can remember when I was two and a half years old.

RUTH: You cannot.

AUSTIN: I can. I can remember still being in my crib.

RUTH: I doubt that.

AUSTIN: No, really. I can remember. . . .

RUTH: What?

AUSTIN: It's a little racy.

RUTH: Tell me.

AUSTIN: I don't know you well enough.

RUTH: Oh, come on. We're both adults.

AUSTIN: I can remember being wakened in my crib by a strange sound. A kind of soft, rustling sound. And— (*He stops.*) Never mind.

RUTH: Go on. You can't stop now.

AUSTIN: It was my nurse—we had this young nurse. I specifically remember seeing her through the bars of my crib. Standing by the window. In the moonlight. Naked. Stroking her body. And I lay there watching her.

RUTH: Through the bars of your crib.

AUSTIN: Through the bars of my crib.

(*Pause.*)

RUTH: Austin.

AUSTIN: What?

RUTH (*melodramatically*): I am that nurse.

AUSTIN: No.

RUTH: No. Just kidding.

(*They both laugh.*)

No, we met after college.

AUSTIN: After college, but before I was married.

RUTH: And before I was.

AUSTIN: You are presenting a rather narrow window of opportunity, madam.

RUTH: I know it.

AUSTIN: I got married soon after college.

RUTH: As did I, sir. As did I.

AUSTIN: So we are talking about a moment in our lives when we were both . . . what? Relatively free and clear.

RUTH: That's what we were. Relatively. Free and clear.

AUSTIN: Those moments are rare.

RUTH: They certainly are.

> (*Sounds of the party within.*)
> (MARION *comes out, gray-haired and maternal.*)

MARION (*looking out and around*): Oh! . . . Ah! . . . Oh! . . .
Now that is what I call a beautiful view! (*She calls toward off-stage.*) Roy, just come out here and look at this view! You
can see all of Boston Harbor!

(ROY *comes out hesitatingly. He is grim and cold.*)

See, sweetheart? There's the U.S.S. *Constitution* right over
there, with the lights on the rigging! (*To* RUTH:) Old Iron-
sides! (*Looking out:*) And behind it is Revere Beach! And that
must be Salem to the north. And those little lights way off to
the right might even be Cape Cod. (*To* AUSTIN:) Excuse me,
sir. You look like one of those people who know everything.

AUSTIN: Oh, I'd hardly say that.

MARION: Do you at least know Boston?

AUSTIN: I've lived here all my life.

MARION: Well, then, could you tell me: are those little lights
Cape Cod?

AUSTIN: They are indeed. They're the lights of Provincetown.

MARION: And I imagine on the other side of the building you
can see the Old North Church, and the Charles River, and
the spires of Harvard.

AUSTIN: I imagine you can.

MARION (*taking his arm*): Oh, isn't that spectacular! Look, Roy!
Just look! It's all here, sweetie!

(ROY *moves up reluctantly.* MARION *turns to* AUSTIN.)

And he wants to leave it.

ROY: I have to leave it.

MARION: You don't have to at all.

ROY (*to* RUTH): I have to move south.

MARION (*to* AUSTIN): He doesn't have to at all.

ROY (*to* RUTH): The weather is getting me down.

MARION: Now you'll hear about his arthritis.

ROY: I've got terrible arthritis.

MARION: It's all in his mind.

ROY: Notice how cold it is. Early September and you can already feel the chill.

MARION (*to* RUTH): Are you cold?

ROY: Of course she's cold.

MARION: *I'm* not cold at all.

ROY: Let the lady talk. (*To* RUTH:) Are you cold?

RUTH (*with a glance at* AUSTIN): Actually, since we've been out here, we've been getting warmer.

MARION (*to* ROY): You see? It's all in your mind.

ROY (*to* RUTH): Last night it got down to fifty-eight.

MARION (*to* AUSTIN): He talks about temperatures all day long. He wanders around the house tapping thermometers.

ROY (*to* RUTH): I've got arthritis in my knees and hips.

MARION (*to* AUSTIN): Will he take a pill? Will he submit to medication? He will not.

ROY: I was once a runner.

MARION: He's never gotten over it.

ROY: I ran the marathon six times.

MARION: I had to line up the whole family on Commonwealth Avenue every Patriots' Day, and cheer him on toward the Prudential Center.

RUTH: What's Patriots' Day?

AUSTIN (*to* RUTH): Ah. It's our own special holiday. It commemorates Paul Revere's ride to Lexington and Concord. " 'Twas the eighteenth of April, in 'seventy-five—"

MARION (*taking over*): "—And hardly a man who is now alive / Who remembers that famous day and year. . . ."

AUSTIN: Good for you. (*To* RUTH:) These days we celebrate it by running a marathon.

RUTH: Sounds very Boston.

AUSTIN: What do you mean?

RUTH: Everyone running madly toward an insurance building.

AUSTIN (*laughing*): Ah, well, I look at it in another way. We celebrate a Greek marathon because we're the Athens of America.

MARION: Exactly! (*To* ROY:) Listen to this man, Roy. He knows. He's chosen to live here all his life. (*To* AUSTIN:) I wish you'd tell my husband why.

RUTH: Yes. I'd be interested in that, too.

AUSTIN: Chosen to live here? Oh, I don't think I ever *chose*. I was born here, I've lived here, I've been here, and now I don't think I could be anywhere else.

MARION: That's because it's the most civilized city in America.

RUTH (*To* AUSTIN): Do you agree?

AUSTIN (*bowing to* MARION): I'd never disagree with such a passionate advocate.

MARION: Thank you, sir.

ROY (*to* RUTH): I did the marathon of seventy-eight under four hours.

MARION: She doesn't *care*, Roy.

ROY: I came in six hundred and seventy-nine out of over fifteen thousand registered contenders.

MARION: Roy . . .

ROY: Now I'm paying for it. Now it's bone against bone. You should see the x-rays.

MARION (*to* AUSTIN): He's found this retirement community in Florida.

ROY (*to* RUTH): It has its own golf course.

MARION: It looks like a concentration camp.

ROY: Oh, for chrissake!

MARION: It has gates! It has guards!

ROY: At least I can stagger around a golf course.

MARION (*to* AUSTIN): It's an armed camp. He's moving me from Athens to Sparta.

ROY: At least I'll get exercise. At least I'll be out of doors.

MARION: We'd be leaving our friends, leaving our children . . .

ROY: A man's got to do something. A man can't just sit and grow old.

MARION: Leaving our grandchildren . . .

ROY: Brace yourselves. Here it comes. I sense it coming.

MARION: We have two grandchildren living almost around the corner. (*She opens her purse.*)

ROY: Here come the pictures.

MARION: I just want them to see.

ROY (*walking away*): Watch it. Sometimes she flashes her pornography collection.

MARION (*sitting down, getting out the pictures*): That's not even funny, Roy! (*She shows* RUTH *a picture.*) There. See? Could you walk away from that?

(AUSTIN *stops walking away.*)

I mean, don't you just want to take a bite out of them?

ROY (*warming his hands at the outdoor candle*): They're not interested, Marion.

MARION: You mean *you're* not interested, Roy. (*To the others:*) He doesn't like his grandchildren.

ROY (*coming down*): I like it when they come, I like it when they go.

MARION: He won't help, he won't pitch in.

ROY: You have the instinct. I don't.

MARION: Everyone has the instinct.

ROY (*with increasing passion*): I have the instinct to migrate south! I have the instinct to land on a golf course!

MARION: See what I'm up against?

ROY: And now I have the instinct to go inside and get warm!

MARION (*with equal passion*): All I want to do is enjoy my own grandchildren!

ROY: You can enjoy them after I'm dead!

(*He goes in.*)
(*An embarrassing pause.*)

MARION: Why have I followed that man around all my life? Answer me that. Do I have to follow him to Florida, just so *he* can follow a golf ball around? (*She slaps her knees.*) My knees are fine! There's nothing wrong with *my* knees. (*She gets up, starts out.*) One of these days he might look over his shoulder and find *me* running my *own* marathon! Right back here. To this wonderful city. And that perfectly marvelous view!

(*She looks at the view one more time, glances at* AUSTIN *and* RUTH, *and then hurries in after* ROY.)

Roy! . . . Roy!

(*And she is off.*)
(*Pause.*)

AUSTIN (*to* RUTH): That view may change.

RUTH: Oh yes?

AUSTIN: There is a group—a consortium—which has approached our bank with a serious proposal to turn Boston Harbor into—what is the expression?—a "theme park." Can you imagine? One of the great natural harbors of the New World! These old wharves have already given way to condominia, such as this one. And soon, if the developers get their way, that lovely string of islands, which once guided the great sailing vessels into port, will be transformed into fake Indian encampments and phony Pilgrim villages. We'll be invaded by tourists from all over multicultural America, lining up to see daily reenactments of the Boston Tea Party and the landing at Plymouth Rock.

RUTH: And are you fighting it, tooth and nail?

AUSTIN: No.

RUTH: No?

AUSTIN: How can you fight history?

RUTH: I suppose by making it.

AUSTIN: Yes, well, apparently you and I made our own private chronicle some time ago, didn't we? Where were we?

RUTH: B.M.

AUSTIN: I beg your pardon.

RUTH: Before Marriage.

AUSTIN: Ah.

RUTH: But after college.

AUSTIN: Was I working then?

RUTH: No.

AUSTIN: No?

RUTH: You claimed you were working. But you were really playing.

AUSTIN: You mean, I was taking time out from my obligations at home to serve my country abroad.

RUTH: I mean, you were a very handsome young naval officer steaming around the Mediterranean.

AUSTIN: You mean, I was defending Western democracy against the constant threat of Soviet domination.

RUTH: I mean, you were living it up, while you had the chance.

AUSTIN: Hmmm.

RUTH: Yes. Hmmm. (*Pause.* RUTH *hums a tune: "Isle of Capri."*)

AUSTIN: Is that a hint?

RUTH: Of course. (*She hums a few more bars.*)

AUSTIN: Sing the words.

RUTH: You sing them. (*She hums again.*)

AUSTIN (*singing*): " 'Twas on the Isle of Tra-Lee—"

RUTH: Wrong.

AUSTIN: " 'Twas on the Isle of Capri that I met her . . ."

RUTH: Right.

AUSTIN: The Isle of Capri?

RUTH: Right.

AUSTIN: Let's see . . . Capri . . . Our ship came into Naples . . . and a bunch of us had liberty . . . so we took a boat out to the Isle of Capri.

RUTH: And?

AUSTIN: And . . . God, let's see . . . we saw the Blue Grotto, and we took a cable car or something. . . .

RUTH (*singing*): "Funiculì, funiculà . . ."

AUSTIN: We took a funicular up some hill. And there was a restaurant on top. And we had some beers. . . . (*It begins to come back*.) And at the next table was a bunch of American girls who were touring Italy. . . .

RUTH: Marsh Tours. See Italy in ten days. Summer Special for the sisters of Sigma Nu from the University of Southern Illinois.

AUSTIN: I struck up a conversation with a girl named . . . Ruth!

RUTH (*Italian accent*): Bravo!

AUSTIN: Hello, Ruth!

RUTH: Hello, Austin.

(*They shake hands again.*)

AUSTIN: What a memory!

RUTH: For that, at least.

AUSTIN: We got along, didn't we?

RUTH: We did. Immediately.

AUSTIN: I remember cutting you off from the herd—

RUTH: Oh, no. I cut *you* off. From *your* herd.

AUSTIN: Anyway, we ended up out on some terrace . . .

RUTH: Overlooking the Bay of Naples . . .

AUSTIN: Which is one of the great natural harbors of the *Old* World.

RUTH: Sorrento to the south . . .

AUSTIN: Ischia to the north . . .

RUTH: Vesuvius smoking in the distance . . .

AUSTIN: Actually, I think Vesuvius had given up smoking.

RUTH: I suppose it had to. There must have been pressure from the people of Pompeii.

AUSTIN: I should think so.

(*Both laugh.*)
    (*The party within is getting livelier, with livelier music.*)
    (DUANE *sticks his head out. He wears a short-sleeved shirt and high-waisted pants.*)

DUANE: Hi there. I'm Duane.

AUSTIN: Hello, Duane . . .

RUTH: Hello, Duane . . .

AUSTIN: Austin and Ruth.

DUANE: Seem to have lost the wife.

AUSTIN: I don't believe she's here, Duane.

DUANE: Small woman? Maybe a little . . . overemotional? (*He peers over the upstage railing.*) She's been upset lately.

AUSTIN: Oh?

DUANE: Reason is, I don't think she wants me to upgrade.

AUSTIN: Upgrade?

DUANE: I've been shopping around for a new IBM compatible with an Intel 486 processor.

AUSTIN: Ah.

DUANE: I think she'd prefer I stay with my old machine.

AUSTIN: I see.

DUANE: So tonight we meet this VP from Data-Tech out on 128, and the guy's just *bought* one! With a new scanner that would knock your socks off! He starts telling us about it, and my wife just turns tail and walks away.

(RUTH *walks away*.)

AUSTIN: Oh, dear.

DUANE: I keep saying I'll upgrade her, too, if she wants. I'd be glad to upgrade her. I mean, she's still using DOS 2.0, if you can believe it.

AUSTIN: Oh.

DUANE: I tell her she's back-spacing herself into the Dark Ages.

AUSTIN: Ah.

DUANE: Well, she's in the files somewhere. I'll just have to search and locate, that's all. I've checked the bar, now I'll check the bathroom. I mean, she may not appreciate a premium machine, but she sure appreciates premium vodka.

AUSTIN: We'll keep an eye out for her, Duane.

DUANE: Thanks, guys. (*He starts out, then stops.*) Say. You folks look like PowerBook users.

AUSTIN: What?

DUANE: Just point and click, am I right?

RUTH: That's one way of putting it.

DUANE: Well, you're way ahead of my wife. She's still hung up on Wordstar 2000. Won't install WordPerfect. Refuses even to touch the mouse!

(DUANE *goes off.*)

AUSTIN (*to* RUTH): Touch the mouse?

RUTH: Skip it.

AUSTIN: Maybe we'd better . . . Let's sail back to the Bay of Naples.

RUTH: Yes. Quickly. Let's.

AUSTIN: Suddenly I want to know . . . Did I . . . ?

RUTH: Did you what?

AUSTIN: Did I kiss you on Capri?

RUTH: Yes, you did.

AUSTIN: I did?

RUTH: Oh, yes. Almost immediately.

AUSTIN: I was a horny bastard.

RUTH: You seemed so. Yes.

AUSTIN: What else did I do?

RUTH: You talked.

AUSTIN: I talked?

RUTH: You said things.

AUSTIN: Did you say things?

RUTH: No. Not really.

AUSTIN: What did you do?

RUTH: I listened.

AUSTIN: I talked, you listened?

RUTH: Primarily.

(*They are sitting down by now.*)

AUSTIN: Was I drunk?

RUTH: A little.

AUSTIN: I used to get smashed whenever I went ashore.

RUTH: Smashed or not, you seemed dead serious.

AUSTIN: About you?

RUTH: About yourself.

AUSTIN: Good God.

RUTH: I don't think I've ever heard anyone else say the things you said. Before or since. That's really why I remembered you.

(*More party sounds; moody jazz music.*)
        (NANCY *comes out, carrying a plate of food and a bottle of beer. She wears slacks and might have a Louise Brooks–style hairdo. She might speak with a Long Island lockjaw accent.*)

NANCY: They have food in there. . . . Don't let me interrupt, but they have food. (*She shows them her plate.*) See? Food. (*She looks at it.*) I think it's food. (*She tastes it.*) Yes. It's definitely food. (*She noisily drags the chaise downstage.*) Don't think I'm antisocial, but someone else is joining me, so I'll sit over here. (*She gets settled.*) Continue your conversation. Don't mind me.

AUSTIN (*to* RUTH): Are you hungry?

RUTH: Not really. Are you?

AUSTIN: Not yet.

RUTH: Why rush for food?

AUSTIN: I agree.

(*Pause.*)

NANCY (*looking at her food*): I don't know what this is exactly. It looks like chicken. Shall I taste it? I'd better taste it. (*She tastes it.*) Yes. This is definitely chicken. In a kind of cream of curry sauce. (*She takes another bite.*) And there's dill in this. Just a tad of dill. It's quite good, actually. I recommend it. (*She begins to eat.*) But please: go on with what you were saying. You both look terribly intense.

AUSTIN (*To* RUTH): How about another drink?

RUTH: No thanks. I'm fine.

AUSTIN: Sure?

RUTH: Absolutely.

AUSTIN: People drink less these days.

(NANCY *is chugalugging her bottle of beer.*)

RUTH: Some people.

(*Pause.*)

NANCY: I don't know where my companion is. We were having a perfectly pleasant conversation, and she said, "Oh, there comes the food. Let's get food," so we got into line, and I thought out here we might be able at least to sit *down*. So here I am. (*She looks off.*) But where is *she*?

AUSTIN: I imagine it's quite crowded in there.

NANCY: It is. It's a mob scene.

RUTH: Maybe your friend got lost in the shuffle.

NANCY: Maybe she wanted to get lost . . . or maybe she wanted *me* to get lost.

AUSTIN: Oh, I doubt that.

NANCY: You never know. People can be very peculiar. It's too bad, though. I thought I was getting on with this one. I thought we clicked.

(AUSTIN *looks at her, is a little taken aback, then turns to* RUTH.)

AUSTIN: Are you cold?

RUTH: Oh, no.

AUSTIN: It's not summer anymore. That's why people are staying indoors.

RUTH: I think it's fine.

AUSTIN: Tell me if you're cold. We'll go in.

RUTH: Do you want to go in?

AUSTIN: No, I don't. Do you?

RUTH: No, I really don't.

AUSTIN: If we went in, we might get lost in the shuffle, too.

RUTH: Exactly.

(*Pause.*)

NANCY (*eating something else*): Now *this* is a vegetable casserole. That's all this is. Zucchini, of course. (*She sticks her tongue out.*)

And tomatoes. A bean or two. It's all right. It'll pass. C minus, I'd say. If that. (*She takes a bite of bread.*) But the bread is good. Very chewy. It would be better with butter. No one serves butter in Boston anymore. But still, it's fine. (*She continues to eat.*)

AUSTIN (*to* RUTH): So. You were saying . . .

RUTH (*softly*): Wait.

AUSTIN: We were talking about—

RUTH (*putting a hand on his arm*): Just wait.

AUSTIN: I'm always waiting.

RUTH: I know.

AUSTIN: You *know*?

RUTH: That's one of the things you told me on Capri.

AUSTIN: I told you that?

RUTH: Ssshh.

(NANCY *is now looking at them.*)
    (*Pause.*)

NANCY (*crumpling up her napkin*): Well, that's that. (*She puts her plate aside, gets up.*) That is definitely that. That was very pleasant. Of course, it might have been slightly *more* pleasant if I hadn't had to eat alone. I mean, she was right behind me in the line. And then she just disappears. It was really very rude. (*She opens her compact, puts on lipstick.*) Are you two married?

AUSTIN: Oh, no. God, no. No.

NANCY: I thought you might be married and were having a fight.

AUSTIN: No, no.

NANCY: Are you lovers, then?

RUTH: No.

NANCY: Be frank.

RUTH: No, we're not.

NANCY (*hovering over them*): Then you're arranging an affair, aren't you? You're arranging an assignation.

AUSTIN: No, we're not doing that, either. I don't think we're doing that. (*To* RUTH:) Are we doing that?

RUTH: I don't know. Are we?

AUSTIN: I think we're just talking.

RUTH: That's right. That's all. Just talking.

AUSTIN: Just two old friends, catching up.

NANCY (*looking them up and down, then focusing particularly on* RUTH): I see. Well. Life has taught me this: even if the main course is somewhat disappointing, there's always dessert.

(*She goes out.*)
    (*Pause.*)

AUSTIN: A rather disconcerting woman.

RUTH: I'll say.

AUSTIN: We might have been a little rude to her.

RUTH: Rude?

AUSTIN: We didn't . . . bring her in.

RUTH: I didn't want to bring her in.

AUSTIN: We should have.

RUTH: Why?

AUSTIN: It was the polite thing to do.

RUTH: Oh, hell.

AUSTIN: I worry about these things.

RUTH: That's because you went to prep school.

AUSTIN: No, not just because of that. I believe in civility.

RUTH: Being from Boston . . .

AUSTIN: Well, I do. The more the world falls apart, the more I believe in it. Some guy elbows ahead of me in a line, I like to bow and say, "Go ahead, sir, if it's that important to you." Treat people with civility and maybe they'll learn to behave that way.

RUTH: It's been my experience that they'll feel guilty and behave worse.

AUSTIN: Well, I feel guilty now. Because I wasn't polite.

RUTH: I feel fine.

AUSTIN: You do?

RUTH: Yes, I do. Because we were doing something very rare in this world that is falling apart. We were making a connection. That's something that happens only once in a while, and less and less as we get older, so we shouldn't let anything get in its way.

AUSTIN: Okay, Ruth. I'll buy that. Okay.

(*Sounds of party laughter from within.*)
(DUANE *sticks his head out again.*)

DUANE: Hi there again.

AUSTIN: Hello . . . ah . . .

DUANE: Duane.

AUSTIN: Duane.

RUTH: Duane.

DUANE: Thought you folks should know: I found the wife.

AUSTIN: In the bathroom?

DUANE: In the kitchen. The caterer was feeding her coffee.

AUSTIN: Uh-oh.

DUANE: No, no. Everything's batched and patched. (*He glances off.*) She's right there in the hall, having a quiet conversation with an old friend from Wellesley. (*He waves to her.*)

AUSTIN: I'm glad, Duane.

DUANE: You see, what we did was sit right down at the kitchen table and talk things over.

AUSTIN: Sounds very wise.

DUANE: Sure was. We put our cards on the table. And I suddenly retrieved the fact that today's her birthday!

AUSTIN: Really!

DUANE: No wonder she was upset. There I was, yakking away about the 486, and she just wanted personal recognition.

AUSTIN: Why don't you buy her a present, Duane?

DUANE: Right. Hey, how about a gift certificate to Radio Shack? . . . Just kidding. . . . No, I'm a romantic guy if you push the right buttons. In fact, I already have a present for her.

AUSTIN: Already?

DUANE: What I did was telephone the kids immediately, and tell them to modem into the new twenty-four-hour nation-wide home shopping free delivery channel. Tonight, when we get home, my wife is going to find one dozen long-stem red roses waiting in the bedroom, personal note attached.

AUSTIN: That might do it.

DUANE: It sure should. Maybe I'm learning something in my old age. (*Calling off:*) Right, honey? Maybe I'm finally learning that women like to be put in their own special subdirectory! . . . Honey? (*To* AUSTIN *and* RUTH:) Pardon, folks. Once again the wife seems to have scooted off the screen.

(DUANE *goes off.*)

AUSTIN: I have the terrible feeling that our future grandchildren will be able to respond to Duane more than to anyone else at this party.

RUTH: Austin.

AUSTIN: Hmmm?

RUTH: Tell me. Did it ever happen?

AUSTIN: Did what ever happen?

RUTH: What you told me about. On Capri.

AUSTIN: What did I tell you about, on Capri?

RUTH: I guess it never happened.

AUSTIN: You've lost me, Ruth.

RUTH: When we had our long talk, you told me you had this problem.

AUSTIN: I did?

RUTH: You did. You said you had a major problem. That's what I remember most about the whole evening. That's really why I wanted to talk to you again. I had to know how it came out.

AUSTIN: What was my problem?

RUTH: Want me to say it?

AUSTIN: Sure.

RUTH: You won't be embarrassed?

AUSTIN: I hope not.

RUTH: You said—and I can quote you almost exactly—

AUSTIN: After all these years?

RUTH: After all these years. . . . You said that you were sure something terrible was going to happen to you in the course of your life.

AUSTIN: Did I say that?

RUTH: You did.

AUSTIN: Something terrible?

RUTH: That's what you said. You said you were waiting for it to happen. You said you'd already spent most of your life waiting.

AUSTIN: What? All of twenty-two years? Just waiting?

RUTH: You said it again ten minutes ago.

AUSTIN: Oh, well . . .

RUTH: No, but that's what you said. You said that you were sure that sooner or later something awful was going to descend on you and ruin your life forever.

AUSTIN: God. How melodramatic.

RUTH: It didn't seem so, then.

AUSTIN: You took me seriously?

RUTH: Absolutely.

AUSTIN: I must have been bombed out of my mind.

RUTH: I'm not so sure. . . .

AUSTIN: And I must have been trying to snow you.

RUTH: Maybe . . .

AUSTIN: I mean, there we were, on the Isle of Capri, over-looking the Bay of Naples . . . me, ashore on liberty after ten days at sea . . . you, an attractive young girl . . .

RUTH: Thank you.

AUSTIN: I must have been trying to snow the pants off you.

RUTH: Well, if you were, you succeeded.

AUSTIN: I did?

RUTH: You most certainly did. In fact, after we got back to the mainland, I invited you up to my room.

AUSTIN: Come on! Surely I'd remember that!

RUTH: The reason you don't remember it is, you said no.

AUSTIN: I said no?

RUTH: Or rather, no thank you.

AUSTIN: And did I give a reason for saying no thank you?

RUTH: Oh, yes. You said you couldn't get involved, because of your problem.

AUSTIN: What?

RUTH: You said you liked me too much to drag me into it.

AUSTIN: I said that?

RUTH: I swear. You said you liked me very much, you liked me more than anyone you'd ever met, and therefore you had to say goodnight.

(*Pause.*)

AUSTIN: I must have been drunk as a skunk.

RUTH: By then you were sober as a judge.

AUSTIN: Hmmm.

RUTH: So. You gave me a big kiss goodnight and went back to your ship.

AUSTIN: And what did you do?

RUTH: Well, if you remember, everybody else was hanging around the hotel bar, drinking beer. . . .

AUSTIN: Did you do that?

(*Pause.*)

RUTH: No.

AUSTIN: No?

RUTH: I went out on the town with a friend of yours.

AUSTIN: A friend?

RUTH: Another officer.

AUSTIN: Who?

RUTH: Oh, Lord, I don't remember. I think he had an Irish name.

AUSTIN (*immediately*): Denny Doyle? Assistant gunnery officer on the forward turret?

RUTH: That could have been the one.

AUSTIN: Denny Doyle? That son of a bitch! He's from Boston, too, you know. He came back and ran for the state legislature!

RUTH: I'll bet he won.

AUSTIN: He sure did. He had every cop in South Boston in his hip pocket. . . . Oh, Christ! You did *Naples* with Denny *Doyle*?

RUTH: I didn't feel like rejoining the "herd."

AUSTIN: That guy was a mover from the word go!

RUTH: He was full of life, I'll say that.

AUSTIN: He was full of bull!

RUTH: Well, he was fun.

AUSTIN: I don't think he ever told me he took you out.

RUTH: I'm glad he didn't.

AUSTIN: He must have thought you were my girl.

RUTH: For a moment there, I thought I was.

AUSTIN (*bowing to her*): I apologize, madam. For turning such a lovely lady down. And leaving her to the lascivious advances of Denny Doyle.

RUTH: Well, you had your reasons.

AUSTIN: Apparently I did.

RUTH: I'll never forget it, though. What you told me. I've met lots of men with lots of lines before and since—but no one ever told me anything like that.

AUSTIN: Some line. What a dumb thing to tell anyone.

RUTH: Oh, no. It worked, in the long run.

AUSTIN: It worked?

RUTH: It's made me think about you ever since.

AUSTIN: Really? More than Denny Doyle?

RUTH: Much more. Particularly when . . .

AUSTIN: When what?

RUTH: When terrible things happened to me.

(*Pause.*)

AUSTIN: *Now* would you like a drink?

RUTH: No thanks.

AUSTIN: Actually, I would.

RUTH: I'll bet you would.

AUSTIN: Shall we go in while I get a drink?

RUTH: You go in, if you want.

AUSTIN: I'm not going to leave you out here alone.

RUTH: Why not?

AUSTIN: It's rude.

RUTH: Oh, nuts to that.

AUSTIN: You're not cold?

RUTH: Not at all.

AUSTIN: Then I'll be back. (*He starts in.*)

RUTH: Austin . . .

(*He stops.*)

How do I know you're not retreating back to your ship?

AUSTIN: Because I'm older now.

RUTH: Which means?

AUSTIN: Which means I learn from my mistakes.

RUTH: That's good to hear.

(AUSTIN *starts in again, then stops.*)

AUSTIN: Will you be here when I get back?

RUTH: Sure. Unless Denny Doyle shows up again.

AUSTIN: He just might. He's now head of the Port Authority, and wild as a Kennedy.

RUTH: Then you better hurry.

AUSTIN: I will. And I'll get us both drinks.

(*He goes.*)

    (*Pause.* RUTH *settles onto the chaise, looks out. We hear the party within, with more sentimental music now in the background.*)

    (TED *and* ESTHER *come out. They wear bright colors and have southern accents.*)

TED (*to* RUTH): Hi there. We're the McAlisters.

RUTH: Hello, McAlisters.

ESTHER: Ted and Esther.

RUTH: I'm Ruth.

TED (*as they look at the views*): We just moved north six months ago.

ESTHER: Can't you tell from how we talk?

TED: We're trying to make the most of Boston.

ESTHER: It's a fascinating experience.

TED: We thought it would be a stuffy old town.

ESTHER: You know: stuffy New England . . .

TED: But it's not at all.

ESTHER: It's different, it's exciting. No wonder they call it the New Boston.

(*They come down to* RUTH *on the chaise.*)

TED: We're making a point of meeting everyone at this party.

ESTHER: And everyone has a story.

TED: If you can just find out what it is. For example, we met this man, a perfectly ordinary-looking man, who turns out to be a real Indian—

ESTHER: Native American, honey.

TED: That's right. A Tuscarora, actually.

ESTHER: He teaches history at Tufts.

TED: Think of that. A Tuscarora chief. Teaching history at Tufts. And there he was, drinking a dry martini.

ESTHER: Teddy said, "Be careful of the old firewater."

TED: And he laughed.

ESTHER: He did. He laughed.

TED: Oh, yes. And we met a couple who travels to Asia Minor every year.

ESTHER: To do archaeology.

TED: So I said, "Maybe we should all talk Turkey."

ESTHER: They didn't laugh.

TED: He did. She didn't.

ESTHER: Oh, well. She's from Cambridge.

TED: And we met several Jewish people.

ESTHER: They're all so *frank*.

TED: That's because they've suffered throughout history. You'd be frank, too, if you'd suffered throughout history.

ESTHER: Oh, and there's an African-American woman in there. Who writes poetry.

TED: And we met this Hispanic gentleman—

ESTHER: Latino, honey. He prefers Latino. And he wants to—shall I say this, Ted?

TED: Sure, say it, we're among friends.

ESTHER: He says he wants to become a woman.

TED: Said he was seriously thinking about it.

ESTHER: Can you imagine? Of course, they say the Boston doctors are the finest in the world.

TED: He may have been pulling our leg.

ESTHER: I know. But still . . . I mean, ouch.

TED: And we met a woman from Cambodia, and a man from Peru—

ESTHER: He looked like an Astec prince.

TED: Half-Astec, anyway.

(*Both laugh.*)

ESTHER: Anyway, he had a story. Everyone has a story.

TED: What's your story, Ruth?

RUTH: Mine? Oh, gosh. That would take years. Are you prepared to sit down and listen to all three volumes?

(TED *and* ESTHER *immediately pull up chairs.*)

ESTHER: Are you a Bostonian, at least?

TED: At least tell us that.

RUTH: Oh, no. That's the last thing I am. I'm just visiting my friend Judith. She's the Bostonian. She moved specially from New York to play in the symphony.

ESTHER: We *met* her! She plays the viola?

RUTH: That's the one.

TED: We met her! She's a little . . . nervous, isn't she?

RUTH: Oh, she just gets upset when things get out of tune.

TED: She thinks things are out of tune?

RUTH: She sure thinks I am.

ESTHER: Where are you from, Ruth?

RUTH: Originally? Oh, well, I was born in the Midwest, but I've kind of kicked around over the years.

TED: And now?

RUTH: And now you might say I'm circling over Logan Airport. Wondering whether to land.

TED: Do it. Come on in.

ESTHER: It's a real nice place to live.

RUTH: That's what Judith says. She thinks I could use a little stability.

ESTHER: Why?

RUTH: Oh, she thinks I court disaster.

TED: That must mean you're married.

(*Everyone laughs.*)

ESTHER: Are you?

RUTH: Four times.

TED: Hey, we're talking to a veteran here.

RUTH: Twice to the same man.

ESTHER: Oh, my.

RUTH: He was very . . . persuasive. (*Pause.*) Still is.

TED: We're talking to a real veteran here.

RUTH: I was married to my first husband for only seven days.

ESTHER: Mercy! What happened?

RUTH: Bad luck. He was killed in Asia.

ESTHER: A real veteran here. A veteran of foreign wars.

RUTH: Korea. Long after the war. A land mine exploded. And he just happened to be there.

ESTHER: Oh, dear.

RUTH: It was just bad luck, that's all. Just very bad luck.

ESTHER: That's a sad story. But at least it's a story. You see? Everybody has a story.

TED: Any children, Ruth?

RUTH (*after a pause*): One daughter. (*Pause.*) Not by him. (*Pause.*) By my second husband. (*Pause.*) You don't want to hear this.

ESTHER: No, we do, we do.

TED: If you want to tell us.

(*Pause.*)

RUTH: We lost her. (*Pause.*) To leukemia. (*Pause.*) When she was eleven years old.

TED: It must be terrible to lose a child.

ESTHER: It must be the worst thing in the world.

RUTH: It is. It's . . . hell. (*Pause.*) We brought her home. She died at home. That . . . helped.

ESTHER: You and your husband pulled together. . . .

RUTH: Yes, we did. We pulled together. But when she was gone, we had nothing left to . . . pull. So we pulled apart.

ESTHER: Oh, dear.

RUTH: But . . . life goes on.

TED: It does, Ruth. It definitely does.

RUTH: So I married a man of the West.

ESTHER: Number three?

RUTH: And four.

ESTHER: Oh my.

TED: He's a cowboy?

RUTH: He thinks he is. . . . He'd like to be. . . . He drives a Ford Bronco.

TED: At least he buys an American vehicle.

RUTH: Oh, yes. He's very—American.

ESTHER: Do you like the West, Ruth?

RUTH: The answer to that is yes and no. (*Pause.*) I'm a little at sea about that. (*She looks out.*) Maybe I'll find new moorings in Boston Harbor.

ESTHER: We're all wanderers, aren't we?

TED: Ships that pass in the night.

RUTH: Some are. (*She glances off to where* AUSTIN *has gone.*) Some aren't. (*Pause.*) Lord knows I am.

TED: I didn't think we would be. But we are now.

ESTHER: We got sent here from Atlanta by his company.

TED: Out of the blue. Just pick up stakes and go, they said.

ESTHER: We didn't want to go at all.

TED: We thought we'd freeze to death, to begin with.

ESTHER: But finally we just said what the hell.

TED: We held our noses and jumped, and here we are.

ESTHER: We got an apartment on Marlborough Street. . . .

TED: Surrounded by students . . .

ESTHER: And we've taken the Freedom Trail.

TED: And we walk to the Gardner Museum. . . .

ESTHER: And Symphony Hall . . .

TED: And we even got mugged once. . . .

ESTHER: All he took was our Red Sox tickets—

TED: And we're taking a course in Italian at the Harvard Extension—

ESTHER: "Nel mezzo di mia vita . . ."

TED (*quietly, seriously*): That's Dante. "In the middle of my life."

ESTHER (*looking at him tenderly*): Which is the way we feel. In the middle of our lives.

(*They nuzzle each other.*)

TED: I think everyone over fifty should change their life, Ruth.

RUTH: Oh, well. I've done that, all right. That I have definitely done. Trouble is, I keep doing it.

TED: We were in a rut before, I'll tell you that.

ESTHER: We were. Maybe we didn't remarry, but we sure re-made our bed.

TED: Now it's more fun sleeping in it.

ESTHER: Oh, now, Ted . . .

TED: The sex has perked way up.

ESTHER: Ted, please . . .

TED (*slyly*): The South shall rise again!

ESTHER: Teddy!

TED: So welcome to Boston, Ruth. It's a great town.

RUTH: I hope you're right.

(AUSTIN *comes back, carrying two drinks in one hand and two plates of food in the other.*)

AUSTIN: I'm back.

RUTH: These are the McAlisters.

TED: Ted and Esther.

AUSTIN (*bowing*): Austin here.

ESTHER (*checking her watch*): Actually, we've got to go.

TED: Right you are. (*To* AUSTIN *and* RUTH:) We made reservations.

ESTHER: There's a place on Route One where you dance.

TED: The old kind of dancing. And not too Lawrence Welky, either.

(*They begin to demonstrate.*)

ESTHER: And the new. We do the new, too.

TED (*demonstrating*): We do disco.

ESTHER (*demonstrating*): We've learned some new moves.

TED: Some students taught us.

RUTH: Sounds like fun.

TED: Say, want to join us?

(RUTH *looks at* AUSTIN.)

AUSTIN: Oh, I don't think so. Not tonight, thanks.

RUTH (*to* TED *and* ESTHER): We haven't seen each other in years, and we're trying to catch up.

AUSTIN: Thank you very much for asking us, though. Thank you.

ESTHER: Next time I want to find out *your* story, Austin.

AUSTIN: I don't have a story.

RUTH: Oh, yes you do.

ESTHER: Of course you do.

TED: Everyone has a story.

RUTH: Austin has a special story.

ESTHER: Well then, get him to tell it.

RUTH: I'm working on that.

TED: Goodbye, you two.

RUTH: Goodbye, McAlisters.

ESTHER: Ciao!

AUSTIN: Goodbye all.

(TED *and* RUTH *go off.*)

That must be what they call the New South.

RUTH: They sure fit into the New Boston.

AUSTIN: I suppose every place is getting pretty much the same these days. Like airports.

RUTH: No. Boston seems different.

AUSTIN: In what way?

RUTH: Well. For one thing, it has you.

AUSTIN (*laughing*): I suppose I am peculiar to these parts. Like baked beans. Though I hope I don't produce the same results. (*He hands her a drink.*) I brought you a vodka and tonic.

RUTH: Thank you.

AUSTIN: Is that what you were drinking?

RUTH: It is now.

AUSTIN: I thought, one last echo of summer.

RUTH: Yes.

AUSTIN: And food. In case you were hungry.

RUTH: Looks delicious.

AUSTIN: There's more sumptuous fare within. But I tried to select what Julia Child tells us is a balanced diet.

(*They sit.*)

RUTH: It all looks fine.

(AUSTIN *takes silverware and a couple of paper napkins out of his pocket.*)

AUSTIN: Silverware . . . and napkins.

RUTH: You're a thoughtful man, Austin.

AUSTIN: Try to be, try to be.

(*Pause.*)
  (*Sounds of the party within: quieter talking and more lush, romantic music.*)

RUTH: So.

AUSTIN: So.

RUTH: So it never happened.

AUSTIN: What?

RUTH: The terrible thing.

AUSTIN: Oh, that.

RUTH: It never happened?

AUSTIN: Oh, no. God, no. No.

RUTH: You never made some terrible mistake?

AUSTIN: Not that I know of. No.

RUTH: You were never hit by some awful doom? Things always worked out?

AUSTIN: Absolutely. I mean, I think so. I mean, sure. After the Navy, I came back. Went to the business school. Got a good job with the Bank of Boston. Married. Married the boss's daughter, actually. Two kids. Both educated. Both launched. Both doing well. Can't complain at all.

RUTH: Sally said you were divorced.

AUSTIN: Oh, well, that . . . (*Pause.*) That doesn't . . . She wasn't . . . We weren't . . . (*Pause.*) She fell in love . . . *claimed* she had fallen in love . . . with this . . . this *creep*. I mean, the guy's half her age! . . . So she got her face lifted. Dyed her hair. Does aerobics on demand. . . . I mean, it's pathetic.

RUTH: So that's not the terrible thing?

AUSTIN: Her leaving? Christ, no. That was a good thing. That was the best thing to happen in a long, long time.

RUTH: And nothing else even remotely terrible happened in your life?

AUSTIN: I don't think so. (*He looks for some wood to knock on.*) At least, not yet.

RUTH: You still think something might?

(AUSTIN *looks off into space.*)

Austin? Hello?

(*He looks at her.*)

Do you?

(*Pause.*)

AUSTIN: I think it all the time.

RUTH: Really?

AUSTIN: All. The. Time. (*Pause.*) I've been very lucky, you know. Too lucky. From the beginning. It's not fair. Something's bound to . . . (*Pause.*) Want to know something?

RUTH: What?

AUSTIN: I'm on Prozac right now.

RUTH: You are?

AUSTIN: It's a drug. It calms you down.

RUTH: Oh, I know Prozac. I know what it does. And doesn't do.

AUSTIN: I don't tell people I'm on it. But I am.

RUTH: Does it help?

AUSTIN: Yes. . . . No. . . . A little.

RUTH: You shouldn't drink with it.

AUSTIN: I don't. Normally. That was a Perrier I was drinking before.

RUTH: But not now?

AUSTIN: This is a white wine spritzer. Tonight I'm becoming very reckless.

RUTH: Be careful. You might make some terrible mistake.

AUSTIN: Sometimes I wish I would. At least the shoe would drop.

(SALLY *comes out, carrying a sweater. She goes to a light switch.* AUSTIN *gets to his feet.*)

SALLY: Let's have some light on the subject. . . .

(*The outside light comes on.*)

You two seem to be having a perfectly marvelous time.

AUSTIN: We are indeed, Sally.

SALLY (*to* RUTH, *holding out a sweater*): Judith thinks you should wear your sweater.

RUTH: Oh, I'm not cold.

SALLY: Well, Judith thinks you will be.

RUTH: Judith is very solicitous. (*She takes the sweater.*) But I'm perfectly fine. (*She doesn't put it on.*)

SALLY: Did you two ever figure out where you met?

AUSTIN: We did. It was very romantic.

SALLY: Oh, good. But it doesn't have to be. (*She starts gathering up plates.*) I met my sweet, dear Ben after class, in Room 120 of Eliot Hall, when I was auditing his course on Renaissance architecture. He was a superb teacher, he knew everything in the world, but I remember thinking, all during his lectures, "I can teach *him* a thing or two." So I married him, and did.

AUSTIN: I took Ben's course.

SALLY: Everyone took Ben's course. Those were the days when we all tried to learn the same things. (*She starts out, then stops.*) Oh. Which reminds me. There's a little man in there from the Berklee School of Music who has been sniffing around Ben's old Steinway. So when things settle down, we're going

to dust it off and try singing some of the old songs. It's probably hopelessly out of tune—*we're* probably hopelessly out of
tune—but that's just a risk we'll have to take.

(*She goes out.*)
  (*Pause.*)

RUTH: I like it here. (*She moves upstage, tosses her sweater
somewhere.*)

AUSTIN: Boston?

RUTH: My friend Judith says it's very livable. The universities,
the music . . .

AUSTIN: My family has had the same two seats at Symphony
Hall for four generations.

RUTH: I'm sure.

AUSTIN: Maybe you'd join me some Wednesday evening. If you
stay.

RUTH: I'd like that. If I stay. (*Pause.*) One thing that scares me,
though. About Boston.

AUSTIN: What's that?

RUTH: Is it a little . . . well, Puritan.

AUSTIN: Whatever that means.

RUTH: Shouldn't do this, have to do that.

AUSTIN: Ah. Yes. Well, some people say there's that.

RUTH: Are they right?

AUSTIN: Puritan? Oh, well. I'm a little . . . close to it. You're
probably a better judge.

RUTH: I sense it a little.

AUSTIN: With me?

RUTH: A lot.

(*Pause.*)

AUSTIN: You sound like my shrink.

RUTH: What? You go to a psychiatrist?

AUSTIN: She's the one who prescribed the Prozac.

RUTH: I can't see you with a psychiatrist.

AUSTIN: Neither can I. My kids conned me into it. After the divorce, I happened to be feeling a little . . . well, glum . . . so they gave me two sessions as a Christmas present.

RUTH: Good for them.

AUSTIN: I went so I wouldn't hurt their feelings.

RUTH: And you've stayed so you wouldn't hurt the psychiatrist's feelings.

AUSTIN: Right.

RUTH: God, Austin! You're so polite! When you die, you'll probably say excuse me.

AUSTIN (*laughing*): Maybe so. (*Pause.*) Anyway, it doesn't work. Psychiatry. At least for me. It may work for them—the younger generation. They're so much at home with all that lingo. And they're all so aware of their own feelings. I mean, they strum on their own psyches like guitars. So it probably works for them. I hope it does. After all, their life is ahead of them. But me? Even if I . . . could say . . . even if I found some way of . . . I mean, it's a little late, isn't it?

RUTH: Don't say that. You should never say that.

AUSTIN: Anyway, she hasn't a clue. My psychiatrist. Not a clue.
I sit there in this hot room on Copley Square, overlooking
Trinity Church, trying to explain. But she hasn't the foggiest.
It was all so different. The world I came from. It was a totally
different culture. All those . . . surrogates. That's what she
calls them. Surrogates breathing down your neck. Nurses.
Cooks. Maids. Gardeners. Aunts and uncles. Parents, too, of
course. And godparents. Grandparents. *Great*-grandparents, for
chrissake. All this pressure. Vertical and horizontal. You were
like a fly caught in this very intricate, very complicated spi-
derweb, and if you struggled, if you made a move, if you even
tweaked one strand of the web, why, the spider might . . .
(*Pause.*) Anyway, what does she know about a world like that?
My shrink. She grew up in a cozy little nuclear family in some
kitchen in the Bronx.

RUTH: Nuclear families can be explosive.

AUSTIN: I'd take a good explosion over death by spider. Caught
in that web, being systematically wrapped in silk, carefully
preserved, until you can't . . . breathe.

RUTH: Oh, now . . .

AUSTIN: Anyway. Puritan. She says I have a Puritan sense of
damnation.

RUTH: Oh, yes?

AUSTIN: She says I've inherited a basically Calvinistic perspective
from my forefathers in Salem and points north.

RUTH: She says that, does she?

AUSTIN (*settling back on the chaise*): Let's see. How does it go? I've been brought up all my life to think of myself as one of the elect.

RUTH: I see.

AUSTIN: But it's hard to feel elect in a diverse and open-ended democracy. Particularly after George Bush lost the election.

RUTH: So?

AUSTIN: So therefore I'm terrified that I may actually be one of the damned, exiled forever from the community of righteous men and women.

RUTH: Isn't that what they used to call predestination?

AUSTIN: Oh, yes. But she says I'm constantly struggling against it. That's why I'm so polite. I'm trying to propitiate an angry God before He lowers the boom.

RUTH: She's got all the answers, hasn't she? This shrink.

AUSTIN: Oh, well. She went to Radcliffe.

RUTH: And this is what I get if I move to Boston?

AUSTIN: We like patterns here. We like categorizing things. Even our subway system is carefully color-coded. The good guys ride the Red Line.

RUTH: I'm someone who likes to ride anywhere I want.

AUSTIN: Right! And I'm full of bullshit.

RUTH: Austin! Watch your language. They'll sentence you to the ducking stool.

AUSTIN (*laughing*): Hey, this has been good. I feel good now. You've got me talking about these things. I've never done that before.

RUTH: Except with your shrink.

AUSTIN: It's different with you.

RUTH: You never talked about it with your wife?

AUSTIN: Oh, God no. Not with her. Never.

RUTH: Maybe that's why she left.

AUSTIN: Maybe. And maybe that's why you've stayed.

RUTH: Maybe.

AUSTIN: See? I've been snowing you again, just as I did on the Isle of Capri.

RUTH: Oh, is that what you've been doing?

AUSTIN: Has it worked?

RUTH: Oh, yes. It's worked all over again.

AUSTIN: I'm glad.

(*He leans over and kisses her. Behind them the sky is a deep, starry blue, as it was in Naples.*)
    (*Then* WALT *comes out, a little drunk. He wears a navy blazer with a crest on it, and gray flannels.*)

WALT: Austin! Sally tells me you've found a— (*He sees the kiss.*) Whoops. Sorry to interrupt.

(*He goes off.*)

RUTH: Who was that?

AUSTIN: That was my friend Walt.

(WALT *comes back on again.*)

WALT: I heard that. "My friend Walt." I like that. "My friend Walt" . . . (*To* RUTH:) I happen to be his best friend in the entire free world.

AUSTIN: That's true. He is.

WALT: Damn right it's true. (*To* RUTH:) We roomed together at Groton. We had a suite together in Dunster House. I was his best man when he married the lovely Cynthia Drinkwater, of Marblehead, Mass. (*He starts to leave.*) Anything you want to know about this guy, just ask me.

RUTH (*more to* AUSTIN): Is he saved or damned?

WALT (*coming back*): Say again?

RUTH: Is he as good a man as I think he is?

WALT: Better. Austin is—and I now quote from the Groton School yearbook—a prince among men.

AUSTIN: Thanks and goodbye, Walt.

WALT: No, and I'll tell you why, uh . . .

RUTH: Ruth.

WALT: Ruth . . . He hails from one of the finest families in the Greater Boston area. As a banker, he has unimpeachable credentials. As a father, he is fair to a fault. As a husband, he is . . . was . . . gentle, thoughtful, and ultimately forgiving. As a friend, he—

AUSTIN: Cut it out, Walt.

WALT: No, Ruth should know these things. You have been occupying Ruth's time, you have been preventing the rest of us from enjoying the pleasure of Ruth's company, you have obviously been attempting to lure Ruth into your bed—has he been doing that, Ruth?

RUTH: No, he hasn't.

AUSTIN: Yes I have.

RUTH: News to me.

AUSTIN: The Lord moves in strange and devious ways.

WALT: Then Ruth should know what she's in for. So I'll tell you this, Ruth. You are about to go to bed with a great squash player. He'd be nationally ranked in the over-fifties bracket, except he won't play outside of Boston. But put this guy in a squash court and you'll see his true colors.

AUSTIN: Ruth doesn't care about squash.

WALT: I'll bet Ruth does. Because Ruth knows, in her deep heart's core, that good at squash means good in bed.

AUSTIN: Oh, Jesus, Walt. (*He walks upstage.*)

WALT: Would you like me to describe Austin's squash game, Ruth?

AUSTIN: I wish you wouldn't.

RUTH: I wish you would.

WALT: The ayes have it. So. Now the secret to squash—we're talking about squash racquets here—is that you're obliged to be both brutally aggressive and ultimately courteous at the same time. At this, my friend Austin is a master. He will hit a cannonball of a shot right down the rail, and then bow elegantly out of your way so you can hit it back.

RUTH: And what if you don't?

WALT: Then he'll ask if you'd like to play the point over.

AUSTIN: God, Walt.

RUTH: He sounds very special.

WALT: He is, Ruth. Now, as you may know, Boston is a great sports town. We produce champions around here: Ted Williams, Bobby Orr, Larry Bird. And we've also produced Austin.

AUSTIN: This is pitiful . . . pitiful . . .

WALT: No, now listen to me, Ruth. Squash is a very old game. And very British. Henry the Eighth played a version of it at Hampton Court. The British raj played it in India. We Americans picked it up in our Anglophilic days, and naturally made some improvements. But lately the game has come to be considered somewhat obsolete. It is deemed obscure, elitist, and somewhat dangerous. So in an attempt to adjust to the modern world—to accommodate women, to make it more telegenic —they've softened the ball, widened the court, and modified the rules. It is only played the old way in a few old cities: New York, Philadelphia, and of course Boston. And here Austin is still unbeatable. Put him in a clean white box, with thin red lines, and the old rules, and by his squash thou shalt know him.

RUTH: And what happens when he steps out of that clean white box?

WALT: Ah, well. Then he likes to take a cold shower.

AUSTIN (*coming downstage*): Knock it off, Walt! This is embarrassing.

WALT: Okay. Sorry.

RUTH: You like him a lot, don't you, Walt?

WALT: Like him? I love the guy. (*Kissing* AUSTIN *on the cheek:*) I love him a lot.

AUSTIN (*backing away*): Damn it, Walt.

WALT: Hey, it's 1993, man. We can do that now, and not even get called on it.

(*Party sounds.*)
     (JUDITH *creeps out self-consciously, beckoning to* RUTH. *She looks like someone who plays in an orchestra. She wears a plain, dark velvet dress and has rather wild, unruly hair. She speaks with a New York accent.*)

JUDITH (*portentously*): Ruth, there's a telephone call for you.

RUTH: For me?

JUDITH: He's tracked you down.

RUTH: Oh. (*To* AUSTIN *and* WALT:) Excuse me. (*She starts in.*)

JUDITH: Ruth . . . I could easily say you're not here.

RUTH: Um . . . well . . . no.

JUDITH: Or Ruth: now listen. I could simply say you don't want to talk to him. Period. I could say that point blank.

RUTH: No. I'll—talk to him. (*She starts in again.*) Where's the phone?

JUDITH: I don't want to tell you.

RUTH: Where is it, Judith?

JUDITH: In Sally's bedroom.

RUTH: I can at least talk to him.

AUSTIN: Will you be back?

RUTH: Of course I'll be back.

JUDITH: Of course she'll be back. (*To* RUTH:) Come back, Ruth. Rejoin the human race.

RUTH: Yes. That's right. . . . (*She starts out again, then stops, returns, puts her arm around* JUDITH. *To* AUSTIN *and* WALT:) Oh. This is *my* friend. Judith.

(*She goes.*)

JUDITH (*shrugging*): Some friend. I shouldn't even have brought the message. I should have walked right into Sally's bedroom and slammed down the phone.

AUSTIN: I'm afraid you have the advantage on this particular subject.

JUDITH: What? Oh. Sorry. That was him.

AUSTIN: Who?

JUDITH: Her husband. He's a deeply flawed person.

AUSTIN: How? How is he flawed?

JUDITH (*looking from one to the other*): Am I among friends here?

WALT: Sure you are.

JUDITH (*after a moment*): He hit her. That's for openers.

AUSTIN: No.

JUDITH: He *hit* her! She had to hit him back!

AUSTIN: Oh, boy.

JUDITH: She told the whole group.

AUSTIN: What group?

JUDITH: I'm sorry. I'm so keyed up I forgot to play the overture. (*She does some breathing exercises.*) We met in this women's group two summers ago at the Aspen Music Festival. My husband and I played Mozart in the morning, and I signed up for assertiveness training in the afternoon. There was Ruth, dealing with her divorce. I thought we were all making great strides, but in the end she went back to her husband.

AUSTIN: So the group didn't help.

JUDITH: It helped me. I decided to leave mine.

AUSTIN: Oh, dear.

JUDITH: I decided he was a weak man.

WALT: Weak—uh—physically?

JUDITH: Weak musically. Weak on Mozart, weak on Mahler, weak even on "Moon River."

AUSTIN: And this—group had a say in all that?

WALT: These women's groups work, man. (*To* JUDITH:) My wife, Ginny, went to one. It improved her net game enormously.

JUDITH (*to* WALT): There you are. They open new horizons. I learned there's more to life than the string section. I'm now seriously involved with a French horn.

AUSTIN: May we talk about Ruth, please.

JUDITH: Ruth? Ruth was unable to release. I mean, the man is a disaster. Once she almost called the police.

WALT: Oh, Christ. One of those.

JUDITH: You got it. One of those. Still, back she goes.

AUSTIN: To where?

JUDITH: Are you ready? Las Vegas.

AUSTIN: Las Vegas?

JUDITH: He likes to live in Las Vegas.

AUSTIN: I'm unfamiliar with Las Vegas.

JUDITH: So am I, and pray to God I remain so. But that's where they live. Furthermore, he's gone through every nickel she's got. She starts this lucrative little art gallery—creates an oasis of civilization out there—and what does he do but bankrupt her.

AUSTIN: Why is she even talking to him, then?

JUDITH (*with an elaborate, complicated, hopeless shrug*): You tell me.

WALT: The guy must have some hold.

JUDITH: Some hammerlock, I call it.

AUSTIN: What does he do in life?

JUDITH: Do? Do? The man gambles. Period. End of sentence.

AUSTIN: Uh-oh.

JUDITH: And to support his habit, he manages a car-rental business.

AUSTIN: Oh, boy. I can tell you, as a banker, that is a very erratic business.

JUDITH: She says he likes all that. He likes being out on a limb.

WALT: Have you met him?

JUDITH: No, thank God. But she showed me his picture. That's another problem. He looks like the Marlboro man.

WALT: Uh-oh. Better load up your six-shooter, Austin.

JUDITH: Please. No macho stuff. Please. It's her choice. She's got to learn to kick the habit.

AUSTIN: Maybe she will.

JUDITH: From your mouth! I mean, the man's a barbarian! Once he grabbed her television and threw it out the window!

AUSTIN: Good Lord.

JUDITH: While she was watching "Jewel in the Crown."

WALT (*to* AUSTIN): There's the bell, buddy.

AUSTIN: What?

WALT: Your serve, man. Time to make your move.

JUDITH: It's time for everyone to make a move. It's time to make a concerted effort.

WALT: Damsel in distress, pal.

JUDITH: Which is why I brought her here tonight. I wanted to show her what civilized life was all about.

WALT: You wanted to show her Austin.

JUDITH: Austin? Austin was just luck. But when she said she *knew* you, Austin, and when Sally said you were *free*, I thought, YES! At least there's *hope*!

AUSTIN: Hey, gang. Don't paint me into a corner here.

JUDITH: All I know is she's a sweet person, and she's had a rough life, and she deserves a better break than she's had so far. . . . Let me see if I can pry her loose from that goddamn telephone!

(*She goes off quickly.*)

WALT: You like her?

AUSTIN: Ruth?

WALT: Of course Ruth.

AUSTIN: I hardly know her.

WALT: She seems like a good gal.

AUSTIN: She's very . . . simpatico.

WALT: You need someone, buddy.

AUSTIN: I've got someone, buddy.

WALT: Who? Your little friend up in Nashua?

AUSTIN: She's there when I need her.

WALT: I'm talking about more than a dirty weekend in New Hampshire, Austin.

AUSTIN: Oh, are you, Walt?

WALT: Give this one a chance.

AUSTIN: I'm not sure what you mean.

WALT: I mean, Ginny and I have tried to fix you up several times. But you gave those ladies short shift, or shrift, or whatever the fuck the expression is.

AUSTIN: Of course I'll give her a chance. I like to think I give everyone a chance. Why wouldn't I give her a chance?

WALT: Because you're acting like a jerk, that's why.

AUSTIN: What is it with you people in this town? Who do you think I am? Some new boy back at boarding school, being set up for the spring dance? I am a divorced man, Walt! I am a father of two grown children! I'll be a *grand*father any day! At our age, we don't just . . . *date* people, Walt. We don't just idly fool around. Every move is a big move. Every decision is a major decision. You ask a woman out, you take her to dinner, that's a statement, Walt. That says something important. Because there's no second chance this time, Walt. This is our last time at bat!

WALT: All the more reason not to be alone.

AUSTIN: And did you ever think, Walt, did you and Ginny ever think that maybe I *like* being alone? Ever think of that? Maybe I've discovered the pleasures of listening to opera while I'm shaving. And *walking* to work through the Commons—rather than riding that damn train! And having a late lunch with a good book at the Union Oyster House! And reading it in bed at night! Maybe I like all that! Maybe I like feeling free to fart!

(RUTH *comes in, carrying dessert and two demitasses.*)

Excuse me, Ruth.

RUTH: No problem.

AUSTIN: I was just letting off a little—steam.

RUTH: Good for you.

WALT: I'll get back to the party.

RUTH: Goodbye, Walt.

WALT: So long, Ruth. I hope we'll meet again.

RUTH: I hope so, too.

(WALT *goes.* RUTH *sets her plates down.*)

I brought dessert.

AUSTIN (*settling at the table*): Very thoughtful.

RUTH: And coffee.

AUSTIN: Decaf, I hope.

RUTH (*sliding him his cup*): What else.

(*They eat, brownies or something.*)

Mmmm.

AUSTIN: A little rich, isn't it?

RUTH: Well, we deserve it. We were so healthy with the main course.

AUSTIN: Right. In Boston, they'd say we're getting our just desserts.

(RUTH *gives him a weak smile.*)
    (*Pause.*)

Everything all right, by the way?

RUTH: With the telephone call?

AUSTIN: Judith told us who it was.

(*Pause.*)

RUTH: He's at the . . . what is it? The Skyway Lounge, out at the airport.

AUSTIN: What? He's there?

RUTH: He's there.

AUSTIN: And?

RUTH: He wants me to join him.

AUSTIN: When?

RUTH: Now. Right now.

AUSTIN: But you're here.

RUTH: That's right. I'm here. Which is what I said. I said I'm having a very good time right here.

AUSTIN: What did he say to that?

RUTH: He said he could give me a better one, right there.

AUSTIN: Could he?

RUTH: He can be . . . fun.

AUSTIN: Did you tell him about me?

RUTH: No.

AUSTIN: Why not?

RUTH: He might have shown up with a baseball bat.

AUSTIN: I could have dealt with that.

RUTH: Oh, yes? With your squash racquet.

AUSTIN: I would have done something.

RUTH (*touching him*): I know you would have, Austin. (*She gets up.*) I just don't want you to, that's all. (*She looks out.*) He's got two tickets on tonight's red-eye back west. First class. And he wants to order a bottle of champagne to drink while we wait.

AUSTIN: Champagne? At an airport bar?

RUTH: He knows I like it. (*Pause.*) First class, too. He knows I'm a sucker for that. (*Pause.*) And he'll charge everything to *my* credit card.

AUSTIN: Sounds like a nice guy.

RUTH: Oh, he . . . has his problems.

AUSTIN: Sure sounds like it.

RUTH: Of course we all do, don't we?

AUSTIN: Ouch.

RUTH: No, but I mean *we* do. Lord knows I do, too.

AUSTIN: Name one.

RUTH: Him.

AUSTIN: Okay.

RUTH: He's not good for me.

AUSTIN: That's an understatement.

RUTH: But he has some redeeming social virtues.

AUSTIN: Such as?

RUTH: Well . . . for one thing, he loves me.

AUSTIN: Oh, sure.

RUTH: He does. . . . He's never traded me in for some young bimbo. He's never taken me for granted. He loves me. . . . I walk out, I leave him, I say this is it, and what does he do? He telephones all over the country till he finds out where I am. Then he grabs a flight to Boston. Calls me here. Offers me champagne. And begs me to come back. . . . He loves me.

AUSTIN: How can he love you if he hits you?

RUTH: He doesn't hit me.

AUSTIN: I hear he does.

RUTH (*more to herself*): Judith! . . . (*To* AUSTIN:) Once, maybe.

AUSTIN: Once is enough.

RUTH: By mistake.

AUSTIN: Oh, Ruth.

RUTH: It was by *mistake*, Austin!

AUSTIN: Some mistake. That's a big mistake.

RUTH: Sometimes he gets . . . carried away.

AUSTIN: Yes, well, that's not love in my book.

RUTH: Oh, really?

AUSTIN: That has nothing to do with love. Rape, violence, things of that kind—I'm sorry, they elude me. They totally elude me. If that's love, then I'm afraid I know nothing about it.

(*She looks at him as if for the first time.*)
  (*Pause.*)
  (*Sounds of people singing around a piano come from within:*

>   "Oh, we ain't got a barrel of money,
>   Days may be cloudy or sunny,
>   But we'll travel along, singing a song
>   Side by side.")

AUSTIN: Well. How about a song at twilight?

RUTH: Maybe it's better if I just . . . (*She makes a move to go.*)

AUSTIN (*getting in her way*): Ruth.

(*She stops.*)

Tell you what. We'll go to the Ritz Bar, you and I. It's a very pleasant, very quiet place. And *I'll* buy you champagne. And I promise you it will be a better brand than what your Marlboro man comes up with, out at the airport. And I'll pay for it *myself.*

RUTH: Austin . . .

AUSTIN: No, and I'll tell you something else. After we've had champagne, we'll go to my place. If you'd like.

RUTH: Oh, Austin . . .

AUSTIN: No, now I don't want you to feel obligated in any way. But I have a very nice apartment on Beacon Street, and we can walk there, right down Arlington Street from the Ritz. And I have a guest room, Ruth. It's a nice room. With its own bath. I keep it for the kids. You can sleep there, if you prefer. I'll even lend you a pair of decent pajamas.

RUTH: Decent pajamas . . .

AUSTIN: No, now wait. If, when we're there, you'd like to . . . to join me in my room, if you'd care to slip into my bed, naturally I'd like that very much. Very much indeed. But you wouldn't have to. Either way, you'd be most welcome. And if things worked out, why we might . . . we might make things more permanent . . . I mean, it's a thought, at least. And if they don't—well, hell, you should always feel free to leave any time you want.

RUTH: Oh, well . . .

AUSTIN: I mean, we obviously get along. That's obvious. We did on Capri and we do now. Hey, come to think of it, this is a second chance, isn't it? We're back where we were, but this time we're getting a second chance. (*Pause.*) So. What do you say?

RUTH (*kissing him*): Oh, Austin. Austin from Boston. You're such a good man.

(*She starts out.*)
(*The singing continues within.*)

AUSTIN: Where are you going?

RUTH: I don't want to tell you.

AUSTIN: To him?

RUTH: I think so. Yes.

AUSTIN: Why?

RUTH: Why?

AUSTIN: Why him and not me?

RUTH: Oh, dear.

AUSTIN: How can you love that guy?

RUTH: If you don't know, I can't tell you.

AUSTIN (*turning away from her*): You don't think I'm attractive?

RUTH: I think you're one of the most attractive men I've ever met.

AUSTIN: Then it must be my problem.

RUTH: Yes.

AUSTIN: You think it's a crock of shit!

RUTH: No! Not at all. No! I take it very seriously. I take it more seriously than you do.

AUSTIN: You think something terrible is going to happen to me?

RUTH: I think it already has.

AUSTIN: When?

RUTH: I don't know.

AUSTIN: Where?

RUTH: I don't know that either.

AUSTIN: But you think I'm damned into outer darkness?

RUTH: I do. I really do.

AUSTIN: But you won't tell me why.

RUTH: I can't.

AUSTIN: Why not?

RUTH: It's too painful, Austin.

AUSTIN: Do you think I'll ever find out?

RUTH: Oh, I hope not.

AUSTIN: Why?

RUTH: Because you'll go through absolute hell.

AUSTIN: You mean I'll weep and wail and gnash my teeth?

RUTH: I don't think so, Austin. No. I think you'll clear your throat, and square your shoulders, and straighten your tie—

and stand there quietly and take it. That's the hellish part. (*She looks at him feelingly.*) I've got to dash.

(SALLY *enters.*)

Oh, Sally . . . Goodbye . . .

(RUTH *goes quickly.*)
   (*Singing offstage:*

>   "*The bells are ringing*
>   *For me and my gal,*
>   *The birds are singing*
>   *For me and my gal . . .*")

SALLY (*looking after* RUTH): That was a little abrupt.

AUSTIN: She was in a hurry.

SALLY: She certainly was.

AUSTIN: She asked me to thank you for her. She said she had a wonderful time.

SALLY: You're lying, Austin. (*She kisses him on the cheek.*) But you're also very thoughtful and polite. Now if I were you I'd call her up at Judith's, first thing in the morning.

AUSTIN: She's going back to her husband. Tonight.

SALLY: Oh, no.

AUSTIN: Flying back to Las Vegas.

SALLY: No.

AUSTIN: That's what she's choosing to do.

SALLY: I hear he's bad news.

AUSTIN: How could she go back to a guy like that?

SALLY: Maybe she hopes he'll change.

AUSTIN: People don't change, Sally.

SALLY: Maybe they do in Las Vegas.

AUSTIN: Not at our age. We are who we are, only more so.

SALLY: No, Austin. No. I can't agree with that. No. If that were true, I'd still be rattling around Ben's house on Brattle Street, having tea with his colleagues, talking about his books. But I sold the house, Austin, soon after he died. And I gave his books to the Widener. And I moved down here to the harbor, so I could live a different life, with different people, who talk about different things.

AUSTIN: Different they are, Sally. I'll say that.

SALLY: And they keep me *alive*! . . . Oh, Austin, give it a try. Why not go after her?

AUSTIN: Sally . . .

SALLY: I mean it. She can't have gone that far! (*She sees the sweater.*) Look! She even left her sweater! You see? You're in luck! She's even given you a good excuse! Take it to her! Right now! Please!

AUSTIN: Sally, I'm not going to scamper off to some airport bar to deliver some sweater. . . . She can come back any time she wants.

SALLY: Maybe she *wants* to be swept off her feet!

AUSTIN: I'm a little old to be sweeping people off their feet, Sally. Just a little too old for that.

SALLY: Oh, Austin, you're hopeless. (*She begins to clean up the dessert plates.*) Well. Come join the party. We found *The Fireside Songbook* tucked away in the piano bench, and after we've gone through that, there's talk of rolling back the rug and doing some serious dancing!

(*Within, they are now singing:*

> "*In a cavern, in a canyon,*
> *Excavating for a mine . . .*")

(JIM *comes out, lighting his cigarette.*)

JIM: I'm sorry. I'm afraid I have to smoke again.

SALLY: At least you tried, Jimmy.

JIM (*his hand shaking as he lights up*): I went almost the whole evening smoke-free, but now look at me, puffing like a chimney.

SALLY: Well, try again tomorrow.

JIM: Right. (*Sitting down, inhaling deeply:*) Meanwhile, gather ye tumors while ye may . . .

(*The singing continues:*

> "*Oh my darlin', oh my darlin',*
> *Oh my darlin' Clementine . . .*")

I was fine till we started in on that fucking song. It made me think of a cat I had. (*To* SALLY:) Remember my cat, Sal? Clementine?

SALLY (*standing behind him*): Of course I remember Clementine.

JIM (*to* AUSTIN): But it isn't really the cat at all. It's the association with my friend Dalton. (*To* SALLY:) Remember Dalton, Sal?

SALLY: I remember him well. I liked Dalton.

JIM (*to* AUSTIN): I had a friend named Dalton, and we'd put our cat in the car, and sing to her, driving down to Provincetown. Have you ever sung to a cat?

AUSTIN: Can't say that I have.

SALLY (*stroking* JIM's *hair*): My poor dear Ben loved music.

JIM (*putting out his cigarette*): I'd take the melody, he'd take the harmony. We were fantastic!

SALLY: Ben played all the old songs on that piano. Sigmund Romberg, Rodgers and Hart . . .

JIM (*starting to cry*): Oh, boy. Now look at me. Now I'm starting to cry. . . .

SALLY (*holding him*): Now, Jimmy. Now, now.

JIM: Shit. I'm going to pieces here. I'm totally falling apart.

(*He breaks down, cries unabashedly.* AUSTIN *stares at him, almost hypnotized.*)

Why are you staring? I'm just a sentimental old fag who smokes.

SALLY: Let's go in, Jimmy. It's cold out here.

JIM (*pulling himself together*): You're right. I'm embarrassing you, Sal, in front of your guest. (*He blows his nose, gets up.*)

SALLY (*pulling the chaise back to where it was*): Austin understands, don't you, Austin? (*She hands him Ruth's sweater.*)

AUSTIN (*taking the sweater*): Oh, yes.

SALLY: Everyone in the world loves *some*thing. Am I right, Austin?

AUSTIN: Oh, yes . . . yes . . .

JIM (*taking off the dessert plates and coffee cups*): Still, it's terrible to let go that way. . . .

(*He goes.*)

SALLY (*To* JIM, *as he goes*): Think how much more terrible it would be if you couldn't! (*She blows out the candle, starts out.*) Coming, Austin?

AUSTIN: In a minute.

(SALLY *goes, turning off the terrace light.*)
    (AUSTIN *stands, clutching Ruth's sweater, lit only by the shaft of light coming from indoors. He takes a deep breath, clears his throat, squares his shoulders, straightens his tie, and looks longingly toward the life within, as the lights fade and the singing ends:*

> "*Thou art lost and gone forever,*
> *Oh my darlin' Clementine.*")

(*Slow fade.*)

THE SNOW BALL

To Jack O'Brien
and
Graciela Daniele

The Snow Ball was first produced at the Hartford Stage Company (Mark Lamos, artistic director; David Hawkanson, managing director) in Hartford, Connecticut, on February 9, 1991. It was directed by Jack O'Brien; the set design was by Douglas W. Schmidt; the costume design was by Steven Rubin; the lighting design was by David F. Segal; the sound design was by Jeff Ladman; the choreographer was Graciela Daniele; the ballroom coach was Willie Rosario; and the production stage manager was Barbara Reo. The cast was as follows:

COOPER JONES	James R. Winker
LUCY DUNBAR	Kandis Chappell
LIZ JONES	Katherine McGrath
MR. VAN DAM/BALDWIN HALL	Tom Lacy
JACK DALEY	Christopher Wells
KITTY PRICE	Susan J. Coon
SAUL RADNER	Robert Phalen
JOAN DALEY	Deborah Taylor
OLDER JACK DALEY	Donald Wayne
OLDER KITTY PRICE	Rita Gardner

VARIOUS MEMBERS OF THE COMMUNITY
as children and adults .... Mary R. Barnett, Terrence Caza, Brian John Driscoll, Cynthia D. Hanson, Robert Phalen, Mimi Quillin, Deborah Taylor, John Thomas Waite

The Snow Ball was subsequently produced at the Old Globe Theatre in San Diego, California, on May 4, 1991, and at the Huntington Theatre in Boston, Massachusetts, on September 25, 1991, with much of the same cast. In Boston, George Deloy and Deborah May played COOPER and LUCY. In both these productions, Douglas Pagliotti was the production stage manager.

CHARACTERS
(sixteen actors)

Individual parts:
COOPER JONES
LIZ, his wife
LUCY DUNBAR, his friend
JACK DALEY as a young man
JACK DALEY as an older man
KITTY PRICE as a young woman
KITTY PRICE as an older woman

Multiple parts:
MR. VAN DAM and BALDWIN HALL
SAUL RADNER, WORKMAN, and FRITZI KLINGER
JOAN DALEY, BARBARA FISKE, and RHODA RADNER
GINNY WATERS and TELEVISION INTERVIEWER
BILLY WICKWIRE, TELEVISION CAMERAMAN, and WAITER
CALVIN POTTER, MUSICIAN, and WAITER
HEATHER HEALY and WAITRESS
BREWSTER DUNN, MR. SMITHERS, and WORKMAN
MARY MONTESANO and OTHERS

SETTING

The play takes place primarily in the Cotillion Room, an elegant ballroom in the old George Washington Hotel, in a large midwestern city. There is a sumptuous staircase, a good dance floor, surrounded by small tables and gilt bentwood chairs, and a high Palladian window looking out at a downtown skyline. Snow may be seen through the window as necessary. Props as needed. A rolling table, serving as a blueprint stand at the beginning, may become a desk, a bar, a counter, and so forth.

The play is designed to be performed to recorded music.

The time is today and yesterday.

At rise: A spotlight isolates a young couple, JACK DALEY *and* KITTY PRICE, *dancing elegantly, spinning, turning, dipping, with a wonderful casual ease, to the sounds of a lovely old tune played by a brisk society band. Behind them, through the window, large snowflakes can be seen slowly drifting down.*

COOPER JONES, *a middle-aged man in a raincoat, enters down the staircase, watches them, and then speaks to the audience.*

COOPER: Jack Daley and Kitty Price were the best dancers in town. There is absolutely no doubt about that. It took your breath away to watch them. A kind of special space would emerge around them on the dance floor, as the rest of us would step back to give them room, and then stand around and watch them dance. (*He watches them for a moment.*) Of course, they weren't quite so good when they were dancing with someone else.

(BILLY WICKWIRE *cuts in on* KITTY.)

Kitty would be light on her feet, and follow fairly well, but she'd always get a little lazy, and run into trouble on the turns. . . .

(*We see this.* HEATHER HEALY *comes on to dance with* JACK.)

And the girls used to say, when they danced with Jack, that he was always looking over their shoulders, looking for Kitty, yearning for a time to dance with her again. . . .

(*We see this, too. Then they change partners so that* JACK *is once again dancing with* KITTY. *The other couple disappears.*)

But together Jack and Kitty were unbeatable. For a few years there, in the center of the century, they ruled the roost. They were by far the best at dancing school, the main attraction at all the other parties, and topped even themselves at the Snow Ball. . . .

(*The light fades on the dancers. The music fades into the sound of hammering and power tools, as the lights come up on the Cotillion Room. We see ladders, a worktable with blueprints, as two* WORKMEN *finish up for the day. Through the window upstage can be seen the lights from other downtown buildings, glassy and modern. It is late afternoon, late fall.*)

(LUCY DUNBAR, *also middle-aged, also in an overcoat, hurries in.*)

LUCY (*breathlessly*): Sorry I'm late. Our sweet little bookstore has just been bought out by what is called a chain. Which means they chain us to the checkout counters. I had to plead temporary insanity to get away.

COOPER: I've been looking around.

LUCY: I knew you would. . . . Doesn't it ring a wonderful old bell?

COOPER: A bell, at least.

LUCY: Dancing school?

COOPER: Jack and Kitty . . .

LUCY: The Snow Ball?

COOPER: Jack and Kitty dancing at the Snow Ball. . . .

(*A glimpse of* JACK *and* KITTY *dancing in the shadows.*)

LUCY: We're making the room exactly the way it was, Cooper. Floor, furniture, everything. We had it legally landmarked.

COOPER: I can see.

LUCY: The rest of this hotel, the rest of downtown, the rest of the *world* can be redeveloped to *death* for all I care, but this room stays exactly the same.

COOPER: Good work.

LUCY: I thought you of all people should see.

COOPER: What's that supposed to mean?

LUCY: Well, I mean, you sold the building.

COOPER: The bank sold it.

LUCY: You made the *deal*, Cooper. You were the real estate broker for the whole operation.

COOPER: It's what I do, Lucy.

LUCY: Oh, yes. And you did it. I just hope you made a huge pile of money.

COOPER: I made almost enough to keep two kids in college another term.

LUCY: Well, the point is, a few of us managed to save this room.

COOPER: I'm glad you did.

(*A* WORKMAN *passes by, putting on his coat.*)

WORKMAN: 'Night, Mrs. Dunbar.

LUCY: Goodnight, Eddie.

ANOTHER WORKMAN (*indicating the window*): Starting to snow.

(*They leave.*)

LUCY (*calling after them*): Drive carefully!

(*Pause. They look at each other.*)

COOPER: I'd better get home, too. (*He starts out.*)

LUCY: I'm thinking of bringing it back, Cooper.

COOPER: Bringing what back?

LUCY: The Snow Ball. This Christmas. To reopen this room.

COOPER: Oh, come on . . .

LUCY: And I want you to help me organize it.

COOPER: Why me?

LUCY: I need your clout. You're a civic leader around here.

COOPER: Not these days, Lucy.

LUCY: You ran the Symphony Drive. You did that work for
  the zoo. . . .

COOPER: I don't do dances.

LUCY: You owe it to me, Cooper.

COOPER: *Owe* it to you?

LUCY: And to yourself.

COOPER: Oh, please.

LUCY: You sold your heritage!

COOPER: Oh, for chrissake!

LUCY: Your grandfather *built* this building! Your father kept it going. And you let the whole thing slip through your fingers!

COOPER: Times change!

LUCY: If we let them.

COOPER: Life goes on, Lucy.

LUCY: Life? Is that life out there? In those great, glass buildings? Or in that lonely walk-up I go home to these days? Is that *life*? Or was this life, right here, in this lovely old room?

COOPER: "Was" is the operative word.

LUCY: And could be again. At least for one night.

COOPER: It would never work without Jack and Kitty.

(JACK *and* KITTY *glide through the shadows upstage.*)

LUCY: Then we'll bring them back, too!

COOPER: You're a hopeless romantic, Lucy.

LUCY (*touching his arm*): Me? What about you? I *know* you, Cooper Jones. I used to dance with you, remember?

(COOPER *goes to look out the window.*)

COOPER: It's early for snow.

LUCY: See? It's a good omen.

COOPER: Or a warning.

LUCY: Oh, please, Cooper. Let's do it. Let's put our best foot forward, one last time.

COOPER: Better get home.

LUCY: And I've got to get back to the chain gang. We're doing inventory, God help us. Everything over six months old gets immediately remaindered. Even the Bible will be fifty percent off. (*She starts out.*)

COOPER: Need a ride?

LUCY: No thanks. Gordon at least left me a car. . . . Will you do it, Cooper?

COOPER: Liz would laugh in my face.

LUCY: Well, if she won't dance with you, I will. . . ,

COOPER: I haven't danced in twenty years.

LUCY: It'll all come back, I promise. . . .

(*She hurries off. The lights focus in on* COOPER. *Behind, in a dim light, the Cotillion Room begins to emerge as it once looked. Off to one side, a group of boys gathers in the shadows. They wear white shirts and dark blue suits and shined shoes.*)

BREWSTER DUNN (*calling to* COOPER): Come on, Cooper! You can't get out of it!

BILLY WICKWIRE: No one gets out of dancing school!

FRITZI KLINGER: Unless you get the mumps.

BREWSTER (*clutching his groin*): Aaagh! Which is almost worth it.

(*On the other side, a group of girls begins to gather, all in formal dresses with white gloves and black patent leather shoes. They primp and giggle.*)

BARBARA FISKE: Is it true you hate girls, Cooper?

GINNY WATERS: Or are you just shy?

HEATHER HEALY: He's cute when he blushes.

LIZ (*as a young girl*): Boys never know what to say.

BARBARA: That's why they have to go to dancing school.

COOPER (*becoming a boy*): I'll never go to dancing school. Ever.
If they send me, I'll walk right out and go to the movies.

BREWSTER: Five bucks says you don't.

COOPER: Shake.

(*They shake hands. The handshake turns into Indian wrestling, which
degenerates into a chaotic wrestling match on the floor, as the boys cheer
and the girls squeal and shriek. MR. VAN DAM, the dancing master,
a portly man in tails, appears from the shadows. He taps his walking
stick on the floor for order. The boys quickly break up their fight and
scamper to their seats on one side of the room. The girls hurry to the
other. COOPER, caught in the center without a chair, has to find one.
When things are settled, VAN DAM slowly parades in front of the class,
inspecting it. LUCY, now in a formal dress, has by now joined the girls.*)

VAN DAM: Posture! Posture! Show the world a straight back!
(*He moves up the line.*) I am looking at feet, I am looking at
hands, I am looking at fingernails.

BREWSTER (*to himself*): Oh, Christ. I forgot to pee.

BARBARA (*to herself*): I'm getting a pimple on my nose. It feels
like Mount Monadnock!

VAN DAM: The young ladies, while seated, will keep their heels,
and knees, together, with their hands folded delicately, palms
upward, in their laps.

(*The girls do this.*)

FRITZI (*to himself*): What a waste of time! I could be organizing my comic books.

LIZ (*to herself*): I hate being new at places. Everybody knows everybody, and nobody knows me.

VAN DAM: The young gentlemen, on the other hand, will keep their legs somewhat apart, with each hand resting lightly on each knee, palms downward, in a manly fashion.

(*The boys do this. They begin to communicate with each other.*)

CALVIN (*to his neighbor*): I wanted to bring my dog, but my parents wouldn't let me.

BREWSTER (*indicating the row of girls*): There's plenty of dogs right here.

(VAN DAM *is now taking a furtive slug from a silver flask.*)

HEATHER (*whispering to her neighbor*): Do you realize we're missing the entire "Hit Parade"?

MARY: My little brother's making a list of the songs.

BILLY (*to* COOPER): Why do we have to come here, anyway?

COOPER: My mother says it will make us better husbands.

FRITZI: My father says it will make us better lovers.

(*The others look at him; he shrugs.*)

LUCY (*to another girl*): I just read *Peyton Place.*

MARY: I hear that's a dirty book.

LUCY: Oh, it is! They even take a shower together.

LIZ (*to* BARBARA): My name's Liz. My mother sent me here to make friends.

BARBARA: I have too many friends. But I could squeeze you in on Saturday mornings.

COOPER (*to* BREWSTER): This afternoon, we saw Rita Hayworth in *Gilda*.

BREWSTER: Boiingg!

(VAN DAM *notices* BILLY.)

VAN DAM: Mr. Wickwire, we do not wear white socks to dancing school.

BILLY: I was playing hockey, sir. I hardly had time to change my pants.

(*Giggles from all.*)

VAN DAM: Gentlemen bathe, Mr. Wickwire. Gentlemen change their stockings and their linen. And gentlemen say "trousers" instead of "pants."

BILLY: Yes sir.

VAN DAM: Mr. Cromeier, may I review the music?

(*He exits.*)

BARBARA: I hate boys. I hate their guts.

HEATHER: I wish they weren't so basically grubby.

MARY: You're cheating, Lucy. You're wearing a bra!

LUCY: This is just Kleenex. It doesn't count.

BREWSTER: Who farted? Somebody cut the cheese around here.

(VAN DAM *comes back, tapping his stick.*)

VAN DAM: The young gentlemen will now ask the young ladies to dance.

(*The boys reluctantly cross the floor, jockeying for position.* LIZ *goes up to* VAN DAM, *whispers in his ear.*)

What? . . . Again? . . . Oh, go on.

(LIZ *scurries out.*)

The young gentlemen will bow.

(*The boys bow awkwardly.*)

The young ladies will rise and curtsy.

(*The girls do.*)

Handkerchiefs out. . . . Positions, please. . . . One, two, three . . .

(*The boys take handkerchiefs out of their pockets and put them in their right hands, so as not to soil the girls' dresses.*)

One, two, three, four . . .

(*They assume the dancing position.* VAN DAM *taps his stick again.*)

We will now review the schottische. . . . Music, Mr. Cromeier, if you please.

(*The music begins: some simple two-step, played very slowly. The couples move stiffly, as* VAN DAM, *with his stick, moves among them.*)

Small steps, please . . . And one and two and . . . Gently, please . . . If you young ladies and gentlemen can't learn the simple schottische, how do you ever expect to dance at the Snow Ball?

LUCY (*to* COOPER, *as they dance*): Isn't this fun?

COOPER (*sullenly*): Oh, yeah. Sure. Goody goody gumdrop.

LUCY: No, but just think. Last week, you chased me home from school. And now you're *dancing* with me.

COOPER: I plan to get out, you know. Errol Flynn got out of Nazi Germany, and so will I.

LUCY: But why? Dancing can be a wonderful way of getting to know people.

COOPER: Stop talking, please. I'm planning my escape.

(*They dance.* LIZ, *now in modern clothes, stands at a table. She combs her hair in a "mirror." The music continues under.*)

LIZ (*calling to* COOPER *as he dances*): What's this I hear about reviving the Snow Ball?

COOPER (*coming out of the dance*): What? There's talk of it. Yes.

(*The dancers dance off.*)

LIZ: From Lucy Dunbar, I'll bet.

COOPER (*going through the mail on the table*): Lucy is exploring the idea, yes.

Liz: Ever since her divorce, she's had a bug up her ass.

Cooper: Jesus, Liz.

Liz: Well, she has. And I didn't like that kiss she gave you the other night.

Cooper: She was wishing me a happy birthday.

Liz: Oh, is that what she was wishing?

Cooper: She's recovering from a rough marriage, Liz. They say that guy used to beat her up.

Liz: And how does the Snow Ball solve that?

Cooper: I imagine she wants to be treated like a lady again.

Liz: I imagine she wants to meet another man. (*She gets her bag.*)

Cooper: Where're you going?

Liz: I've got a meeting. Down at the office.

Cooper: At seven in the evening?

Liz: It's the only time we could all meet. There's that macaroni stuff in the freezer.

Cooper: Sounds delicious. (*He reads his mail.*) What's this "lab supplies" for Teddy? I thought he hated science.

Liz: That's a film course. It's called Film Lab. They make films.

Cooper: Two hundred and thirty-five bucks! What's he making? *Ten Commandments Two?*

Liz: Now now.

Cooper: No science, no foreign language, no history. Next term he at least has to take a history course. Agreed?

Liz: Agreed.

COOPER: He who ignores the past is doomed to repeat it.

LIZ: I said I agreed.

(*Pause.*)

COOPER: But you don't like the idea of the Snow Ball.

LIZ: I think it sucks.

COOPER: Liz, hey, your language. You've been working with street people too long.

LIZ (*putting on lipstick*): Well, at least I'm not Lucy Dunbar, digging up dead dogs.

COOPER: She got them to refurbish the Cotillion Room. That's a good thing.

LIZ: I guess.

COOPER: You *guess*? We met in that room. We had our wedding reception there.

LIZ: It was a lovely room. . . .

COOPER: Why not reopen it with a splash?

LIZ: Because no one *dances* that way anymore, Cooper. Kids don't know how to, and grown-ups don't want to.

COOPER: I want to.

LIZ: Oh, come on.

COOPER (*trying to dance with her*): I remember a time when you wanted to.

LIZ (*breaking away*): Cooper, I am late. It's a meeting on homelessness, and I happen to be running it.

COOPER (*watching her get ready*): There's even talk of bringing back Jack and Kitty.

(YOUNG JACK *and* KITTY *are seen dancing upstage.*)

LIZ: Jack and Kitty haven't even *seen* each other in several centuries.

COOPER: Still. There's talk.

LIZ: Don't tell me you're personally involved in all this.

COOPER: I'm thinking about it.

LIZ: Oh, Lord, Cooper. You always go overboard on these things. First it was the philharmonic. Then the zoo . . .

COOPER: I happen to care about endangered species.

LIZ: Well, I'm sorry, but I can't get wound up over some dumb dance while this city disintegrates around us.

COOPER: Maybe you'd like to turn the Cotillion Room into a shelter.

LIZ: Better that than having a bunch of old WASPs waddle around the dance floor!

COOPER: Don't knock your roots all the time, Liz!

LIZ: The hell with roots! Roots hold you down!

COOPER: They also keep you alive.

LIZ: You can't turn back the clock, Cooper!

COOPER: So I'm left to turn on the microwave.

LIZ: Cooper, it's snowing like mad, and I'm already late! (*She starts out.*)

COOPER (*calling after her*): Homelessness begins at home, Liz! (*He picks up telephone, starts to dial.*)

LIZ (*returning*): You made me forget my briefcase. . . . Who're you calling?

COOPER: A friend.

LIZ: Oh.

COOPER: An old friend.

LIZ: Oh.

COOPER: Someone who stays home at the end of the day.

LIZ: Oh, Cooper.

COOPER: Why? Do you care?

LIZ (*kissing him*): Sweetheart, I care about being late at the moment! (*Starts out again.*) Oh, and if you go to bed before I'm back, don't forget to turn down the furnace!

(*She's out.*)

COOPER (*calling after her*): It's already down, toots! I'm worried about the pipes freezing! (*He starts to dial, then turns to the audience.*) I mean, Jesus, how do you like that woman? Everyone says she's bloomed since the kids left home, and she got this job—"Liz has bloomed," everybody says. Okay, okay, she's bloomed, she's a flower, she's a goddamn gardenia—but what about me? No. Wrong. What about *us*? When do we talk, when do we make love, when do we *eat*, for chrissake? (*He starts to dial, then turns to the audience again.*) She wants to move out of this house, you know. Oh, sure. She wants to sell this fine old house and move. Downtown! To some waterfront condo where she can be quote in the thick of things unquote. What about the garden? What about my grandmother's furniture? What about the goddamn dog? "Time to move on," Liz says. "Time to grow." Well, maybe it's time to remember who we are. *(He picks up the phone again.)* My mother says it's roots that count. That's why Liz and I have lasted so long. That's why the kids have turned out so well. Roots, says my mother. Similar backgrounds. Birds of a feather. All that shit.

(Piano music. The ghostly dancers begin to return.)

Well, maybe so. Liz and I sure knew the steps for a while. With each other. With the kids. Maybe that's why I'm hung up on this goddamn dance. I want to glide through the world with a woman again, at least for one night! *(Into telephone:)* Lucy? Hi. . . . It's me. . . . Hey, on this Snow Ball thing—I think it's one hell of a good idea.

(The dancers return, dancing better than before. VAN DAM pounds out the beat with his stick.)

VAN DAM: And one and two and one and two and . . .

(LIZ reappears in her formal dress. She sits in a chair on the sidelines, and then calls to COOPER furtively.)

LIZ: Pssst. . . . Hey, you! . . . Are you Cooper Jones?

COOPER: What's it to you?

LIZ: You're supposed to dance with me.

COOPER: Says who?

LIZ: Says your mother. I'm new in town, and your mother told my mother you'd ask me to dance.

COOPER: News to me. (*He starts to walk away.*)

LIZ: Oh, come on. It's like going to the dentist. It prevents problems later on.

(COOPER *reluctantly goes to* LIZ, *bows in front of her.* LIZ *gets up from her chair, curtsies to him, and then they join the circle of dancers, dancing stiffly around the room.*)

Thank you.

COOPER (*grumpily*): You're not welcome.

VAN DAM: And one and two, and small steps two, and one and two and . . .

LIZ: I hear this town is going rapidly downhill.

COOPER: Wrong!

LIZ: My father says we've climbed aboard a sinking ship.

COOPER: For your information, we're the thirteenth largest city in the United States. And our zoo is internationally famous.

LIZ: All I know is, there are bad slums. Next summer I'm going to be a junior counselor for slum kids.

COOPER: Goody for you.

LIZ: Want to help? They need boys.

COOPER: No thanks. I'm going to tennis camp.

LIZ: You're kind of superficial, aren't you?

COOPER: At least I'm not a do-gooder.

LIZ: At least I care about other people.

COOPER: At least I—are you wearing perfume?

LIZ: Sure. Smell. (*She offers her neck.*) I swiped it from my mother.

(COOPER *furtively sniffs her neck.*)

 Like it?

COOPER: At least you don't have BO.

(*They dance closer.* VAN DAM *notices.*)

VAN DAM: Mr. Jones: just what do you think you're doing?

COOPER: Making quiet conversation, sir.

VAN DAM: Come to the center of the circle, please!

COOPER (*to* LIZ, *under his breath*): Thanks a bunch.

LIZ: I didn't do anything.

COOPER: You seduced me.

VAN DAM: We're waiting, Mr. Jones! The rest of you may take
 your seats.

(COOPER *goes to the center. The other boys and girls sit down.*)

 Please demonstrate the box step to the assembled multitude,
 Mr. Jones.

(COOPER *dances awkwardly by himself, as* VAN DAM *jerks him
around or pokes him with his stick.*)

COOPER (*to audience, in rhythm as he dances*): How could I have
 done this? How could I have done this? Week by week, year
 by year? Was this me, then? Was this really me, then?

VAN DAM (*poking him*): And how do we hold our hands?

(COOPER *holds his hands out appropriately.*)

COOPER: Is this what my roots are? This degrading ritual? Week by week, year by year? (*Breaks out of the rhythm.*) Why didn't I protest against this drunken old fascist? My own sons would have taken one look and headed for the hills! Why didn't I rebel—like Stewart Granger in *Scaramouche*?

(*He suddenly grabs* VAN DAM'*s stick, pretends to run him through, stands over him triumphantly. The others clap. But* VAN DAM *bounces to his feet.*)

VAN DAM: One together, two together . . .

COOPER: Oh, but not me. Oh, no! Me, I volunteered to be a galley slave, like Ben-Hur on a bad day. Why did I accept it? Why did I keep going?

(LUCY *enters on the side, carrying a book, talking furtively on the telephone.*)

LUCY: I can only talk a minute! They're watching me like hawks. But I've managed to call all the old gang, and they say they'll come out of the woodwork for the Snow Ball!

COOPER (*still in dancing school*): We'd look like fools without Jack and Kitty.

LUCY: Slowly, Cooper! Gently! One step at a time, remember?

(*She goes off.*)

VAN DAM (*simultaneously*): . . . One step at a time, remember?

(KITTY PRICE *enters on the staircase, in a shining white dress. She is young and gorgeous—and is to be cast young, the only woman in the dancing class who is close to her stage age.* VAN DAM *sees her, raps his stick angrily on the ground. The music stops. Everyone looks at* KITTY.)

KITTY: Oops. Sorry I'm late.

VAN DAM: Indeed you are, Miss Price. It is becoming a habit with you.

KITTY: I guess I lost track of the time.

COOPER (*aside to* FRITZI): Watch this. He won't dare get mad at her.

FRITZI: Why not?

COOPER: She's the richest girl in town. If she quit, so would everybody else.

VAN DAM: We will overlook it this time, Miss Price.

(COOPER *and* FRITZI *shake hands knowingly.*)

The young gentlemen may now ask the young ladies to dance.

(*All the boys dash across the floor and slide to a stop in front of* KITTY, *who beams proudly.*)

STOP!

(*The boys do.*)

Go back!

(*The boys return to their places.*)

The young *gent*lemen will ask the young *ladies* to dance.

(*This time the boys move more slowly across the floor, elbowing each other out of the way.* COOPER *gets to* KITTY *first. In the process,* FRITZI *gets a nosebleed.*)

BARBARA: Mr. Van Dam! Fritzi has a nosebleed!

VAN DAM: Oh, please.

(*He shoos them off.*)

Handkerchiefs out! A waltz please, Mr. Cromeier!

(*The piano plays a slow waltz.* LUCY *and* LIZ *dance together.*)

Now the waltz is one two three, one two three . . .

LUCY (*to* LIZ): Don't you wish you were Kitty Price?

LIZ: Sometimes.

LUCY: I mean, she's both rich and beautiful.

LIZ: I know. But she's kind of lazy.

LUCY: What makes you say that?

LIZ: I sit next to her in arithmetic. She hardly knows how to divide.

LUCY: She doesn't need to divide. When you're that rich, all you have to do is multiply.

(COOPER *dances with* KITTY.)

COOPER: Will you come to Smithers' drugstore afterwards? I'll buy you a soda.

KITTY: No thank you. I'm being driven straight home so no one will kidnap me.

COOPER: Okay. I'll meet you next Monday after school. I'll show you the zoo.

KITTY: No thanks. I find the monkey house generally embarrassing.

COOPER: Tell you what, then. You can watch me play hockey next Saturday afternoon.

KITTY: I can't. I'm going skiing with my father.

COOPER: Then when can I see you?

KITTY (*as he steps on her toe*): Ouch, Cooper! . . . Maybe when you become a better dancer.

VAN DAM: That is the waltz. . . . We will now take our seats for a slight collation.

(JACK *enters, a young busboy—who is to be cast young—in a white jacket, carrying glasses of pink punch on a silver tray. The boys and girls follow him off.* VAN DAM *exits as well, sneaking a furtive snort from his silver flask. Downstage,* SAUL RADNER *enters as if into his office. He is a real estate developer and wears a business suit. He calls* COOPER *off the dance floor.*)

SAUL: Come on in, Coop. When do we start up our winter squash series?

COOPER: When you learn how to handle my serve.

SAUL: I've handled it for ten years, pal. I think you're scared of my corner shot.

COOPER: That does it! The clash of the Titans resumes next Tuesday! . . . Hey. Dig the new decor. Hard to believe this office once belonged to my old man. (*Picks up a fancy telephone.*) Gimme Donald Trump! Gimme Barbra Streisand!

SAUL: Come work for us, and we'll put one of those in your car.

COOPER: No thanks, pal. No more downtown deals for me. I'll settle for selling houses to my people, as they retreat to the suburbs.

SAUL: That's a good one—your "people."

COOPER: Sure. We're kind of the lost tribe these days, Saul.

SAUL: Bullshit.

COOPER: I'm serious. I feel like an exile. This isn't my territory anymore. All these new buildings. Even the old George Washington Hotel is different.

SAUL: Except for one room.

COOPER: Except for one room.

SAUL: Your "people" on the Landmark Commission cost us a small fortune on that one.

COOPER: Actually, that's why I'm here.

SAUL: I figured. (*He reads a letter on his desk.*) Ms. Lucy Dunbar . . . wants to put on a . . . "Snow Ball."

COOPER: She said you turned her down.

SAUL: I didn't turn her *down*, Coop. I asked her to broaden her base.

COOPER: Broaden her base?

SAUL: When you reopen a public facility, Coop, particularly when federal funds are involved, it's a good idea to kick things off a little more . . . well, democratically.

COOPER: Hey. The Snow Ball is open to anyone who wants to come.

SAUL (*referring to the letter*): Anyone in "formal attire" holding a two-hundred-buck ticket.

COOPER: That's for a New York orchestra and open bar and special decorations and—

SAUL: Forgive me, Coop, but some of our minority citizens might see it simply as the old guard doing their old number at taxpayers' expense.

COOPER: Oh, come on . . .

SAUL: Open it up, Coop. Reflect the ethnic diversity in town. Less liquor, more food. Tacos, pizzas, egg rolls. Throw in a folksinger, maybe a rock group for the kids.

COOPER: That room was designed for ballroom dancing, Saul.

SAUL: I know that.

COOPER: My grandfather had that dance floor imported specially from Austria.

SAUL: I know, I know.

COOPER: Grover Cleveland danced in that room. Irene Castle danced there. Charles Van Dam taught dancing school there for almost fifty years.

SAUL: Coop, the Landmarks Commission gave us the whole history lesson. . . .

COOPER: Well, what's wrong with a little history now and then? Continuity? Tradition? You of all people should understand that. I'll bet if this were a fund-raiser for Israel, you'd be cheering us on.

SAUL: Now wait a minute.

COOPER: I want this, Saul. I want it. I put you up for the Tennis Club. I wrote that recommendation for your son to Williams. Now please. You do this for me.

(*Pause.*)

SAUL: Give your party, Coop.

COOPER: Thanks, Saul.

SAUL: Give your party.

COOPER: Now I assume you'll send us a good, healthy bill for the use of the room. We may be a lost tribe these days, but we still pay our own way.

SAUL: You sure? I hear your office lost out on that new mall.

COOPER: We're doing okay.

SAUL: Seriously, Coop. Come work with me. Together we could get this burg back on its feet. And squeeze in some squash at lunch.

COOPER: Let's talk about it after the first of the year.

SAUL: You mean you're postponing a major career decision because of some *party*?

COOPER: Not a party, Saul. A dance. There's a big difference. This may even involve Jack and Kitty.

SAUL: Who and who?

COOPER: You and Rhoda come see. You're in for a big surprise.

SAUL: Sorry, Coop. We're booked that night. Flying over to Jerusalem for a major dinner party at the Wailing Wall.

(SAUL *goes off, as the boys and girls reenter with* VAN DAM.)

VAN DAM: Concentrate on your conversations, ladies and gentlemen.

(JACK *comes down to* COOPER *with a tray of punch.*)

JACK: Want some punch?

COOPER: Thanks.

JACK (*confidentially*): Say, could I speak to you privately a minute?

COOPER: Sure.

(*They come downstage.*)

JACK: How do I get into this dancing school?

COOPER: Huh?

JACK: I've been watching from the kitchen. I already learned the steps. (*He gives a demonstration; he is good.*)

COOPER: If you know already, why do you want to get in?

JACK: Personal reasons.

(KITTY *comes down to* VAN DAM.)

KITTY: Mr. Van Dam. I have to leave.

VAN DAM: The class is not over, Miss Price.

KITTY (*with a quick curtsy*): I know, but I think I've had enough for one evening. (*She bounces up the staircase.*) Thanks!

(*She goes out.*)

JACK: That's the reason.

COOPER: Kitty?

JACK: I want to dance with *her.*

COOPER: You and the rest of the free world.

JACK: So how do I get in?

COOPER: I don't know exactly. My mother has some list. You have to know people.

JACK: I know you.

COOPER: I don't know you.

JACK: I'm Jack Daley.

COOPER: Cooper Jones . . . Hiya, Jack.

(*They shake hands.*)

And I think you have to pay three hundred dollars.

JACK: I can come up with that.

COOPER: You can come up with three hundred *dollars*?

JACK: I saved it. Working here.

COOPER: Do you have a dark suit?

JACK: I'll get one.

COOPER: Then you definitely should get in. I mean, are we a democracy, or what? I'll ask my mother.

VAN DAM (*tapping his stick; with great distaste*): We will now undergo a lindy hop.

(*Everyone cheers;* VAN DAM *drinks.*)

Music, Mr. Cromeier, if you please.

(*Music begins, a lively lindy.*)

JACK (*dancing off with his tray*): Tell your mother I want to start next Saturday.

(*He goes.*)

COOPER (*dancing with* LIZ): Okay, Jack Daley. (*To* LIZ:) Stop leading. I'm the boy.

LIZ: Then lead, please.

COOPER: I'm trying to. But you keep going your own way.

LIZ: Why do you keep dancing with me, then?

COOPER: I'm practicing for the wrestling team.

VAN DAM: Change partners!

(COOPER *switches to* LUCY.)

LUCY: You dance beautifully, Cooper.

COOPER: Thanks.

LUCY: I'm serious. I can put myself completely into your hands.

COOPER: Thanks.

LUCY: And you'd be even better if you took that thing out of your pocket.

COOPER: What thing? Oh. Gosh. Sorry.

(LUCY *dances off with the others as a* WAITER *sets up a table with two coffee cups.* COOPER *calls off as he moves toward it.*)

Joe! If my secretary calls, tell her I'll be back in ten minutes.

(LUCY *comes back on, in contemporary clothes. They settle at the table.*)

LUCY: I've tracked them down.

COOPER: Jack and Kitty?

LUCY: Both. Since you seem to feel they're so essential.

COOPER: Yep. I do. They're the heart of the matter.

LUCY (*checking her notebook*): Jack is living in Indianapolis with wife and children.

COOPER: I knew that. He sends me a Christmas card every year.

LUCY: I'll bet you didn't know he's running for governor.

COOPER: Governor!

LUCY: According to my cousin, who lives there . . . (*she reads from her notes*) he's assistant district attorney now, and he's being seriously mentioned as the Republican candidate for governor of Indiana!

COOPER: Good old Jack. Still moving on up . . .

LUCY (*consulting her notes*): And Kitty . . .

COOPER: Ah, Kitty . . .

LUCY: Kitty has married again.

COOPER: Again?

LUCY: Number three. A retired banker named Baldwin Hall. They live in this posh resort down in Florida.

COOPER: Oh, boy. We've got our work cut out for us.

LUCY: Exactly. I think we should start by writing them both letters, just to break the ice.

COOPER: Okay. I'll write Jack. You write Kitty.

LUCY: Fine.

COOPER: And tell Kitty I have the music.

LUCY: The music?

COOPER: The musical arrangements. From the Snow Ball. Jack gave them to me when they split up. (*He calls as if for bill.*) Joe!

LUCY: And you kept them? All these years? I *knew* you were a closet romantic, Cooper Jones. (*She pokes him with her pencil.*)

COOPER: Tell Kitty I'll Xerox them and send them on.

(*They get up from the table.* COOPER *leaves money.*)

LUCY: We should work out a budget.

COOPER: Yes.

LUCY: I'm hopeless at budgets. Gordon did all that.

COOPER: Oh, budgets aren't so difficult.

LUCY: Then stop by tonight and show me, step by step.

COOPER: Can't. It's Liz's birthday.

LUCY: Oh. Well. Far be it from me to intrude on *that*. . . .

(*The music and lights come up as the class reenters. Again the dancing has improved.* JACK *dances downstage with* BARBARA FISKE.)

BARBARA: Don't you love dancing cheek to cheek, Jack?

JACK: I don't know. It gets a little sweaty, maybe.

BARBARA: I like that. I think it's sexy.

JACK: I dunno. I think I'm getting a rash.

(COOPER *and* LUCY *are back in by now.* KITTY *enters down the stairs.* VAN DAM *sees her and once again raps for order. The music stops.*)

KITTY: I know, I know. I'm late again. (*She looks around.*) Gulp.

VAN DAM: I believe everyone has found a partner, Miss Price.

KITTY: Then I'll just sit this one out. (*She sits.*)

VAN DAM: Miss Price! (*He approaches her.*) Perhaps you would like to dance with *me*.

KITTY: You?

VAN DAM: (*He bows to her.*) May I have this dance?

(KITTY *does not rise and curtsy.*)

LIZ (aside to HEATHER): The old letch.

HEATHER: What will she *do*?

VAN DAM (*holding out his arms to* KITTY): Music, Mr. Cromeier, if you pl—

JACK (*suddenly*): I'll dance with her.

VAN DAM: I believe you already have a partner, Mr.—ah . . . Mr. . . .

JACK: Daley.

VAN DAM: I believe you are already dancing with Miss Fiske.

JACK: No offense, but she doesn't get the beat. She can't follow me at all.

(BARBARA *bursts into tears and runs to the other girls, who comfort her.*)

Tell you what: *you* dance with Miss Fiske. *I'll* dance with Miss Price.

(*General uproar.* VAN DAM *gets order by pounding on the floor with his stick.*)

VAN DAM: No. I'll tell *you* what, Mr. . . . ah . . . Daley. You will dance with Miss Price. And the rest of us will take our seats and watch.

JACK: Okay.

VAN DAM: And let me add, Mr. Daley, that you had better be very, very good!

KITTY (*to the other girls*): Eeeek.

VAN DAM: Mr. Cromeier, if you please . . . a rumba.

KITTY: A *rumba*? Hey, no fair! We haven't even learned that one!

VAN DAM: Ah, but Mr. Daley will teach you.

KITTY: Yipes.

VAN DAM: Be seated, everyone. . . . Music, Mr. Cromeier, if you please.

(*Music: a rumba.* JACK *gives* KITTY *a beautiful, deep bow.* KITTY *responds with a dramatic, ironic parody of a curtsy. The handkerchief comes out, and then they dance. They dance tentatively at first, finding the beat,* JACK *taking the lead,* KITTY *following, always with a wry little shrug, and always a little bit late. They learn as they go along, and as they learn they get trickier, trying this and that, and the music seems to respond and take fire from what they do. The boys and girls cheer them on, so that* VAN DAM *has to tap his stick and yell, "Settle down! Settle down!" Soon* JACK *and* KITTY *are looking pretty good, building finally to an elaborate coda, where he spins her off in a lovely flourish, and ends the dance with a deep theatrical bow. Everyone applauds. The boys all gather enthusiastically around* JACK *and bring him downstage as the girls gather around* KITTY *and propel her off.*)

(MR. SMITHERS, *a druggist in a white jacket, sets up a counter downstage as* VAN DAM *exits, taking a nip from his flask. The boys do a lot of whooping and cheering and backslapping as they settle in around the table.*)

COOPER: I'm paying for Jack. I got a dollar for shoveling snow.

BILLY: That's not all you shovel, Cooper.

(*Roars of laughter.*)

SMITHERS: What'll it be, boys?

COOPER: You got that new chocolate chip ice cream?

CALVIN: You got cherry phosphates?

FRITZI: You got Prince Albert in the can? If so, let him out!

(*More roars of laughter.*)

BILLY: When we heard the sirens and saw the patrols
      We knew it was Smithers for whom the bell tolls.

(*Laughter.*)

CALVIN: Hey, Mr. Smithers! Have you got that new paperback,
      The Tiger's Revenge, by Claude Balls?

(*Laughter.*)

SMITHERS: All right, boys. Settle down, settle down.

(*He goes off.*)

COOPER: Say, you're a terrific dancer, Jack!

(*Other boys echo approval:* "Fred Astaire!" "Gene Kelly!")

JACK: Thanks for getting me into dancing school.

BILLY: *Thanks?* You said *thanks?* You mean you *wanted* to go?

COOPER: He wanted to dance with Kitty.

CALVIN: I dunno. I don't think even Kitty is worth going to
      dancing school for.

JACK: I had another reason, too. I figure dancing school will be
      good for my future.

FRITZI: Your *future?*

JACK: Sure. You learn things in dancing school. You learn manners. You learn clothes. You learn how to talk to people when you don't give a shit.

FRITZI: That's true. . . .

JACK: Sure. And you meet people. Getting to know you people will help me succeed in life. I figure it's worth three hundred dollars.

BILLY: You mean you're *paying* for it? With your *own* money?

JACK: Sure. I saved it for my college education, but I decided this was an equally important investment.

(SMITHERS *returns.*)

SMITHERS: Who here is Jack Daley?

(*Everyone:* "Ta-da," *pointing out* JACK.)

JACK: Me. Why?

SMITHERS: There's a fellow in a uniform asking to see you.

FRITZI: Jiggers. The cops.

CALVIN: You rob a bank for that three hundred, Jack?

COOPER (*looking out*): That's no cop! That's a chauffeur . . . and Kitty's father's sitting in the back of the car.

ALL: Uh-oh.

SMITHERS: He wants to meet you, son.

JACK: Okay! (*He runs off jauntily.*) So long, suckers!

(*He exits.*)

CALVIN (*looking out*): This I gotta see!

BILLY: It's one of those new Lincoln Continentals!

COOPER: They're shaking hands!

BILLY: He's getting in!

COOPER: They're driving off!

FRITZI (*producing a schoolbook with a brown paper cover*): Hey! Jack forgot his book.

COOPER: What book?

FRITZI: This book he studies on the bus.

COOPER (*taking it, reading the cover*): Tenth Grade Civics. Holy Angels Collegiate Institute. (*He reads inside.*) *How Democracy Works.*

BILLY (*looking after* JACK): It sure is working for *him.*

(*The boys go off, leaving* COOPER. *Restaurant music comes up. The lights become more romantic. A* WAITER *brings on a table with a cloth and a candlestick.* LIZ *comes in, breathlessly late, wearing an overcoat. She kisses* COOPER.)

LIZ: Sorry, sweetheart. . . . What with a late meeting, and the snow, and . . .

COOPER (*helping with her coat, which the* WAITER *takes*): Happy birthday. . . . (*He gives her a warm kiss.*)

LIZ: Thanks. (*She settles in.*) Susie called as I was going out the door. She wants to stay at college over Thanksgiving, and put her travel money toward a used car.

COOPER: No.

LIZ: That's exactly what I said. No.

COOPER: The children come home Thanksgiving and Christmas. That's absolutely nonnegotiable.

LIZ: I couldn't agree more.

COOPER: Can you imagine you and me all by ourselves, eyeing each other over a Thanksgiving turkey?

LIZ: I suppose we'll have to face that someday.

COOPER: Not if I can help it.

WAITER (*reappearing*): A cocktail, madam?

LIZ: Just club soda, please.

COOPER (*indicating his own drink*): You won't join me?

LIZ: No thanks.

COOPER: How about champagne? On your birthday?

LIZ: Champagne gives me a headache. (*To* WAITER:) Just club soda, please.

(WAITER *goes off.*)

COOPER: I've decided on your present.

LIZ: Oh, yes?

COOPER: You've got to pick it out.

LIZ: I hope it's not jewelry, Cooper. I can't wander around town dripping with jewels while people are sleeping in the streets.

COOPER: It's not jewelry. . . . It's a new dress.

LIZ: Cooper, I'm not sure I need a—

COOPER: A long dress. For the Snow Ball.

LIZ: Oh.

COOPER: I checked out Berger's. I saw a great dress there. The salesgirl held it up. You'd look sensational in it.

LIZ: Describe it.

COOPER: Well, it has a . . . and a little . . . Oh, hell, it's dark green. You'll have to go see.

LIZ: How much?

COOPER: Never mind.

LIZ: How much, Cooper?

COOPER: Four hundred smackeroos.

LIZ: Four *hundred* dollars?

COOPER: Including tax.

LIZ: That is outrageous! To pay four hundred dollars for some dumb dress, when the library closes three days a week!

(*The* WAITER *shows up with the club soda.*)

Nope. Sorry. I'll wear some old rag, thanks. . . . I suppose we should order. (*She looks at the menu.*)

COOPER: I've already ordered. Something special.

LIZ: What?

COOPER: Rack of lamb.

LIZ: Lamb?

COOPER: And fresh asparagus.

LIZ: Sweetheart, lamb is saturated with fat.

COOPER: It is not.

LIZ: Darling, it's oozing with it. And do you know what they do to these baby lambs in order to—

COOPER: Oh, Liz . . .

LIZ (to WAITER): Could I just have the . . . I don't know . . . scrod, broiled, no butter, and a small green salad with dressing on the side.

WAITER: Certainly, madam.

COOPER: I'll have the goddamn lamb.

WAITER (to COOPER): What about the soufflé, sir?

COOPER (to LIZ): I ordered the Grand Marnier soufflé for dessert.

LIZ: Oh, that sounds wonderful! (To WAITER:) I'll have a taste of his.

WAITER: A single soufflé then?

COOPER: A single soufflé.

LIZ: And herb tea, for me.

COOPER: Not even decaf?

LIZ: Do you know what those coffee companies pay their peasants in Peru?

COOPER: Help.

(The WAITER goes off.)

LIZ: The reason I was late was we had this knock-down, drag-out meeting at the office. They want to give the holiday party down at the Community Center the Saturday after Christmas.

COOPER: But that's the night of the Snow Ball!

LIZ: I _know_, darling. I fought it tooth and nail. But it's the best date for everyone else.

COOPER: So what gives? You're not coming to the Snow Ball?

LIZ: I'll just have to make a showing at both.

COOPER: Say you've got a previous engagement. You've done it before.

LIZ: I can't this time, sweetheart. . . . I've been promoted.

COOPER: No kidding! When?

LIZ: Last week.

COOPER: Why didn't you tell me?

LIZ: Because I was nervous about what you'd say.

COOPER: What I'd say?

LIZ: It'll take much more time.

COOPER: Will you come home Thanksgiving and Christmas?

LIZ: See? That's what I was nervous about.

COOPER: No, seriously. Congratulations! (_He kisses her._) What's your title?

LIZ: I am now known as a family interventionist. I intervene, when necessary.

COOPER: You'll be great at that.

LIZ: Well, we could use the dough, sweetie. With the kids in college and all.

COOPER: Right. So. For your birthday, what would you like? Is there an *Interventionist's Handbook?* Or how about a four-volume history of the Marshall Plan? Name it. It's yours.

LIZ: No, listen, here's what I'd really like. Computer lessons. To learn how to work one of those things. I could use it in the office, and maybe get one for home, and I could get twice as much done in half the time. . . .

(*The lights fade on* LIZ *as she talks and come up on* LUCY, *across the stage, sitting at a bar, with two glasses of white wine in front of her. She hails* COOPER.)

LUCY: Hey! Yoo-hoo! Over here!

(COOPER *crosses to her.*)

COOPER (*glancing around*): Hey, how'd you find this joint? The Half Moon Bar and Grille?

LUCY: Where else should we meet? Your precious club? With everyone breathing down our necks? No thanks. It's time you branched out a little, Cooper Jones. (*Indicating the wine:*) And I've already ordered you a drink.

COOPER: In the middle of the day?

LUCY: Absolutely. I think you and I should spend this entire snowy afternoon stuffing our faces with greasy chicken wings and getting pleasantly polluted.

COOPER (*sitting beside her*): What's the trouble?

LUCY: My job, for one thing. They just chewed me out for talking to the customers. They say I flirt with the men.

COOPER (*mock horror*): What? You? I don't believe it.

LUCY: I like men. I like talking about books. I don't know why I can't combine the two.

COOPER: Why don't you quit?

LUCY: Money, Cooper. Believe it or not, there are some people in the world who need it. Besides, it's a place to go. Anyway, look what finally arrived from Kitty.

COOPER: Better late than never.

LUCY: Not when you read what she says.

COOPER (*reading*): "I couldn't possibly drag Baldwin north in the dead of winter—"

LUCY: Baldwin's her husband.

COOPER: "And we're expecting a houseful of children and step-children and grandchildren over Christmas vacation. . . ."

LUCY: See?

COOPER: Shit.

LUCY: And to make things worse, Jane Babcock tells me she just ran into her at the Mayo Clinic. She was having tests. Jane didn't dare bring up the Snow Ball.

COOPER: Hell.

LUCY: So that's that. . . . Anything new from Jack?

COOPER: Just what I told you. I wrote two letters, and got two polite put-downs from some assistant in his office.

LUCY: So where are we?

COOPER: Nowhere. (*He stares at Kitty's note.*)

LUCY: So. Let's talk about books. What have you read lately? *The Decline of the Wasp?*

COOPER (*rereading Kitty's note*): Hey!

LUCY: What?

COOPER: Did you read this last sentence?

LUCY: What?

COOPER (*reading*): "Just think. Another Snow Ball. Jeez Louise. My heart automatically goes thumpety-thump. . . ."

LUCY: Typical Kitty.

COOPER: She's giving us an opening, Lucy.

LUCY: The size of a pinhole.

COOPER: She is beckoning to us. She is calling. She's saying "Tell me more."

LUCY: Oh, Cooper . . .

COOPER: I sense it. I feel it in my bones.

LUCY: So what do we do?

COOPER: We telephone them both. Immediately.

LUCY: You mean just—

COOPER: Call them up. Person to person. Tell each one that the other is on the fence.

LUCY: But that wouldn't be . . .

COOPER: All's fair in love and dancing! I'll call Jack, you call Kitty.

LUCY: Heavens, Cooper. You certainly are taking the bit in your teeth.

COOPER: Faint heart ne'er won fair lady.

LUCY: But if she's sick?

COOPER: If she says so, we'll back right off. (*He gets up.*) Come on. We'll go over to my office and telephone.

LUCY: Could we make it my place?

COOPER: Why?

LUCY: I'm expecting a call. From Minneapolis. From this man. Well, I mean, he's a welcome change from that prick who held me hostage for twenty years. (*Pause.*) He keeps wanting to marry me.

COOPER: And why don't you?

LUCY: Because he's not . . . I mean, he wouldn't . . . I mean, something like the Snow Ball is totally out of his league.

COOPER: Aha.

LUCY: So. Let's go to my place. If Minneapolis calls, I'll say I'm otherwise engaged.

(*Pause.*)

COOPER: I have to show a house this afternoon.

LUCY: Oh, well. A house . . .

COOPER: Money, Lucy. Remember? I haven't been holding my end up at the office lately.

LUCY: Oh, well. I wouldn't want to take bread from the mouths of your children. We'll call separately.

(COOPER *puts down money.*)

No, no. My turn.

(LUCY *puts her money on top of his; their hands touch and stay touching.*)

After all, we're both in this thing together.

COOPER (*bowing and offering his arm*): Shall we dance?

LUCY (*curtsying*): You must have gone to dancing school, sir. Which is more than I can say for my man from Minneapolis.

(*She goes off.* COOPER *turns to the audience.*)

COOPER (*to audience*): It wasn't that great, actually. Not at the start. Maybe because it really wasn't about us. It was all about Jack and Kitty. They were on our minds that afternoon, and those other afternoons when we met again. It was as if we were just the subplot, two minor characters marking time, until the stars were ready to come on and play their big scene.

(LUCY *comes on, dressed informally.*)

LUCY: I just thought you should know: Ruthie Curtis saw Kitty at Bergdorf's in New York. Buying an evening dress!

COOPER: For the Snow Ball?

LUCY: She wouldn't say. But it was not the sort of thing you'd wear to some golf club in Florida!

(*They kiss.*)

COOPER: I finally got through to Jack. He said he hasn't danced in thirty years.

LUCY: Did you tell him it will come back?

COOPER: I said it was like riding a bicycle.

LUCY: Exactly. Like that, or other things.

(*They kiss more passionately; then* LUCY *breaks away.*)

Hey! Slow down. I'm right in the middle of a good book.

COOPER: What book?

LUCY: *Lady Chatterley's Lover.*

(*She goes off invitingly.* COOPER *turns to the audience again.*)

COOPER: So things got better, as we got closer to the Snow Ball. Jack and Kitty were still on the fence, but we began to feel that by making love, we could copulate them into commitment. In our more lurid moments, we even joked about it. We called it "Snow Balling" . . .

(SAUL RADNER *crosses the stage, in shirtsleeves, carrying a squash racquet, drying his hair with a towel.*)

SAUL: Good game, Coop. You're hotter than a pistol these days.

COOPER: Thanks, Saul.

SAUL: You been exercising on the sly?

COOPER: No, no. Just generally keeping fit.

SAUL: No, it's more than that. You seem like a guy who's got a girl somewhere.

(COOPER *laughs nervously as* SAUL *goes off, passing* LIZ *on the way in.*)

LIZ (*holding a little pink note*): Look what I got in the mail!

COOPER: What?

LIZ: An anonymous note. "Interventionist: intervene thyself."

COOPER: Some crank. Some weirdo from your work.

LIZ: On pink writing paper? With that little face at the end? It's someone we know.

COOPER: But the grammar's wrong. "Intervene" is an intransitive verb. It should be "intervene *on* thyself." Or "*with* thyself." It's some uneducated kook.

LIZ: At least it has a biblical ring. . . . I'll look it up in Bartlett's. . . .

(*She goes off.*)

COOPER (*looking after her; then to audience*): Oh, God, what a shit I am! What a shit! Because I love her! I love her even when I argue with her. I love her even *because* I argue with her. She keeps life interesting every minute of the day. As for Lucy, do I love her, too? Or are we just hung up on the Snow Ball? Am I another one of those menopausal men, desperately trying to turn back the clock before the last alarm goes off?

(LUCY *comes out, in a negligee.*)

LUCY: Where've you been?

COOPER: Kitty's husband called me at the office.

LUCY: And?

JACK: She's in the hospital. For an operation.

LUCY: Oh, no.

COOPER: I telephoned Jack, and he immediately backed off.

LUCY: Oh, no!

COOPER: I wonder if we should back off, too.

LUCY: I know what you mean.

COOPER: I keep thinking of Liz.

LUCY: And the man from Minneapolis.

COOPER: The Snow Ball should keep rolling, of course.

LUCY: Of course. We'll just have to go through the motions.

COOPER: Well. I ought to get back. One of our kids is home for the weekend.

LUCY: Oh, then definitely you should go.

COOPER: So long, then, Lucy. (*He kisses her on the cheek.*)

LUCY: Goodbye, Cooper. (*He starts out.*) Cooper . . . will you still dance with me at the Snow Ball?

COOPER: Of course I will, Lucy.

LUCY: I mean, we may not be Jack and Kitty, but I'd hate to think we spent all those years dancing for nothing.

COOPER: Oh, something will come of this. I'm sure of that.

(*They go off either way, as: The music comes up, bouncily, and plays continuously. Decorations swing into place. We are now at a series of parties, spanning several years. The boys are now in tuxedos, the girls in long dresses. A couple dances by; the girl is in a strapless dress.*)

BREWSTER: How come they call this a coming-out party?

HEATHER (*hoisting up her front*): Wait till the conga and you'll see.

(JACK *and* KITTY *dance by, beautifully. Another couple watches.*)

GINNY: I hear Jack Daley quit that Holy Angels parochial school and is now going to Country Day.

BILLY: That's right. Kitty's father got him a full scholarship.

GINNY: My Lord! Is he doing well?

BILLY: Straight A's! And co-captain on the football team!

GINNY (*suddenly kissing him*): Oh, that Jack! He makes me proud to be an American.

(JACK *and* KITTY *dance by again; people applaud as they dance off. Two boys, with drinks, cross.*)

CALVIN (*confidentially*): I saw Jack last Friday night, out with another girl.

FRITZI: Probably Terri Tolentino, his old girl from Holy Angels.

CALVIN: I thought Jack stayed in Fridays, to do his homework.

FRITZI (*lewdly*): He stays in Fridays, all right. He stays in all night long. (*Quickly, as* JACK *dances on with* LUCY:) Hi, Jack.

JACK: Guys.

LUCY: You're a beautiful dancer, Jack.

JACK: Thanks, Lucy.

LUCY: No, you are. You're fabulous.

JACK: Thanks a lot.

(COOPER *cuts in on* JACK *and* LUCY. JACK *goes off. Music continues.* COOPER *dances with* LUCY.)

LUCY: You're a beautiful dancer, Cooper.

COOPER: Thank you, Lucy.

LUCY: I hear Liz doesn't like you to dance with me.

COOPER: She thinks I'm a pushover for your line.

LUCY: Line? What line? I don't have a line.

(CALVIN *cuts in.*)

COOPER: That's what I told her.

(*He goes off.*)

LUCY (*to* CALVIN, *who dances terribly*): You're a beautiful dancer, by the way.

CALVIN: Hey, thanks.

(*They dance off.* JACK *joins* COOPER *in the men's room.* COOPER *stands at a "urinal."* JACK *combs his hair in a "mirror."*)

JACK: Look at you, Cooper. You're a slob. Your pants don't even fit.

COOPER: That's because this tux belonged to my grandfather.

JACK: I got mine tailor-made. It cost a mint, but I'm buying it on time.

COOPER: Hey, I could have lent you my older brother's.

JACK: No thanks. A man's clothes should fit. If your clothes fit, you feel fit. And if you feel fit, you dance well.

COOPER: And if you dance well? What then?

JACK: Oh, well, my God, then the sky's the limit!

(*They go off either way.* KITTY, HEATHER, *and* GINNY *come into the ladies' room.* KITTY *adjusts her dress.*)

HEATHER (*from "stall"*): There's a boy here from Princeton who says he loves me.

KITTY: Don't believe him.

GINNY (*from next "stall"*): And this guy from Amherst wants to pin me.

KITTY: Watch it. He'll pin you to the ground.

HEATHER (*as they wash their hands*): Oh, God! How do you tell if a man's *sincere*?

KITTY: Dance with him. Let him lead. You can tell immediately.

(*She goes off; the girls look at each other and go off the opposite way.* JACK *dances with* LIZ.)

LIZ: Congratulations, Jack. I hear you got into Harvard.

JACK: Right. And they gave me this great scholarship. Instead of waiting on tables, they want me to dance with Kitty at alumni functions.

LIZ: That's terrific!

JACK: We'll be what the Whiffenpoofs are for Yale!

LIZ: What about Kitty? Where does she stand in all this?

JACK: Oh, she's with me all the way. She's found a college near Harvard which gives lab credit for dancing.

(*They dance off.* BREWSTER *and* HEATHER *dance by.*)

BOY: Do you think Jack and Kitty are sleeping with each other?

GIRL: I don't think it's any of our business.

BOY: I hear they spent all last weekend down at Niagara Falls in the Maid of the Mist Motel.

GIRL: Honestly, Charlie! May we change the subject, please?

BOY: Sure. Go ahead.

GIRL: All right. Now. Here's the thing. I think I'm pregnant.

(*They dance.* COOPER *and* KITTY *dance by.*)

COOPER: When we were little kids, I was in love with you.

KITTY: You were not.

COOPER: I was! I thought you were the cat's ass.

KITTY: I love that expression!

COOPER: I still dream about you sometimes.

KITTY: That's because we're such good old friends.

COOPER: Say, how about coming skiing with me over New Year's?

KITTY: Can't, sweetie. I'll be with Jack.

COOPER: Thank God. I've already invited Liz.

KITTY: What would you have done if I'd said yes?

COOPER: Asked Lucy Dunbar to join us.

(*Both laugh.*)

Do you love Jack, Kitty?

KITTY: Oh, Cooper, I don't know.

COOPER: He's good for you, Kitty. He's given you something to go for.

KITTY: I know. (*She does a little spin.*) But it's hard *work* being Ginger Rogers.

COOPER (*imitating*): It's no cinch being Jimmy Stewart, either.

(GINNY *and* MARY *come downstage to settle at a table. They have white ballots, white envelopes, and white pencils.*)

GINNY: This is agony. . . . Who are you going to vote for, for Snow Queen?

MARY: I think I'll vote for Kitty.

GINNY: But she's so antisocial. She's spent almost the entire vacation down in her rumpus room, alone with Jack.

MARY: Maybe she should just be maid of honor.

(BARBARA *joins them.*)

BARBARA: I'm voting for Agnes Underhill.

GINNY: But Agnes has that gimpy leg. And that horrible skin problem.

BARBARA: I know, but she deserves a sympathy vote. Besides, her cat just died.

(*They vote carefully, hiding their ballots from each other.*)

GINNY: Oh, God. These decisions. I'm just not sure democracy's worth it.

(*They go out.* COOPER *crosses with* LIZ.)

COOPER: I voted for you for Snow Queen.

LIZ: You sure you didn't sneak one in for Lucy Dunbar?

COOPER: No, I swear. You're queen to me, all the way.

LIZ: Whatever that means.

COOPER: I guess it means I'm asking you to go steady.

LIZ: Cooper . . . Gosh. Let me think about that.

COOPER: Let me know at the Snow Ball.

(*She goes off as he turns to the audience.*)

Because it all came down to the Snow Ball. This was the only party you had to pay for, but the profits went to some good cause, and besides, you could always stick your grandmother for the bill. Balls are balls, as my father says; but the climax of this one, like the parading of the Virgin in an Italian street festival, was the presentation of the Snow Queen to the assembled multitude.

(*A fanfare.* VAN DAM *comes down the staircase with a mike on a cord.*)

VAN DAM: Ladies and gentlemen: it is my great pleasure to present to you . . . this year's queen and her court. The beautiful Miss Kitty Price and her two lovely maids of honor.

(*A drumroll. A spotlight on an entrance upstage as* KITTY *is wheeled on in an elaborate sleigh. She wears a crown and holds flowers.* LIZ *and* LUCY *sit below her, as maids of honor.* COOPER *and three other boys pull the sleigh around, as the band plays a swing version of a Christmas song, and everyone applauds. Over the mike:*)

Prance, gentlemen! Prance! You're supposed to be reindeer!

(*The sleigh finally lurches to a stop in the center of the floor. More applause.*)

KITTY (*holds up her hand to speak*): I just want everyone to know this thing is held up primarily by faith in God and Bergdorf Goodman.

(*Laughter.*)

VAN DAM (*holding up his hand*): Ladies and gentlemen: I'd also like a word, please. It has long been observed, by people wiser than myself, that every American city requires two things to keep it civilized: it must have a park, and it must have a dancing school. For forty-six years, I have been somewhat involved in the latter.

(*Laughter and applause.*)

This year, however, will be my last.

(*Genial protests.*)

No, no. My last. Because during the course of this year, I have enjoyed the rare pleasure of seeing my labors bear fruit. I have seen the dancing of Mr. Jack Daley and Miss Kitty Price.

(*Cheers and applause.*)

The escorts will now ask the queen and her court to dance.

(COOPER *goes up, bows to* LIZ, *helps her out of the sleigh.*)

COOPER: So? Are we going steady?

LIZ: Yes, Cooper. If you mean it seriously.

COOPER: Of course I do.

LIZ: Well, let's hope.

(*Another boy escorts* LUCY. KITTY *remains seated in the sleigh.*)

GINNY: Kitty doesn't have a partner!

BILLY: Where's Jack?

BARBARA: Who knows?

FRITZI: Maybe he's over at Terri Tolentino's.

HEATHER: This is embarrassing. Kitty'll have to dance with her father.

VAN DAM (*on mike*): I notice our lovely queen remains unattended. Perhaps, for my last Snow Ball, I might finally have the pleasure of dancing with her myself.

LIZ (*to someone*): He's still an old letch.

(*General confusion.* VAN DAM *goes to bow to* KITTY *in the sled.*)

May I have this dance, Miss Price?

KITTY: Um . . .

(*And everyone freezes.*)

COOPER (*to audience*): Jack, of course, had arranged this whole moment. He wanted the suspense. He had ordered music specially arranged in New York, and dug up some guy who did the lighting for Ringling Brothers, and now he was waiting offstage, ready to make his move.

BILLY: There's Jack. In the orchestra.

MARY: Thank God!

GINNY: He's handing out sheet music!

(JACK *comes on. He nods as if to the orchestra. A long drumroll. He signals to the flies. The lights dim, except for two gorgeous pink spotlights, which hit him and* KITTY. *The drumroll continues. The other dancers back off.* JACK *goes to the sleigh, bows to* KITTY, *holds out his hand, helping her out. She steps down and gives her bemused curtsy.* JACK *signals to two boys, who ease the sleigh out of the way. Then* JACK *gestures again toward the orchestra.*)

JACK: Hit it, Eddie!

(*The band strikes up a snappy arrangement of dance tunes, and* JACK *and* KITTY *launch into a terrific number. They have obviously worked on it carefully, and both the lights and the musical arrangements support what they do.*)

BILLY (*on the sidelines*): No fair. That's cheating. They've been practicing to their own music.

GINNY: So *that's* what they were doing down in Kitty's rumpus room.

LIZ (*to* COOPER): I still think she's lazy. Notice how she's always a little late.

COOPER: At least she *follows* him.

LIZ: That's because he knows where he wants to go.

(*The dance modulates into a slower tempo.* COOPER *and* LUCY *exit unobtrusively.*)

FRITZI (*watching the dancers*): Poetry in motion, that's what it is. Poetry in motion.

GINNY: If they wore skates, they could be in the Olympics.

FRITZI: They make the hair stand up on the back of my neck.

CALVIN: You said that yesterday about the new Thunderbird.

(JACK *and* KITTY*'s dance builds. They might dance up the staircase and freeze on the balustrade.* COOPER *and* LUCY, *both now in contemporary overcoats, enter from either side downstage. They meet somewhere in the center, isolated in light.*)

COOPER: I got your message.

LUCY: Kitty telephoned. She's out of the hospital, and now wants to come more than ever!

COOPER: I'll call Jack immediately! . . . We've done it, haven't we?

LUCY: We're bringing it all back home.

COOPER: Lucy, I want to sleep with you all night long!

LUCY: What about Liz?

COOPER: I'll tell her I got stuck in the snow.

(*They kiss passionately, and go up the stairs, as* JACK *and* KITTY *dance down, building their dance to a rousing climax. At the end, everyone gathers in on them, applauding, including* COOPER *and* LUCY, *who have had time to reenter as their young selves.*)

(*Fade to black.*)

ACT TWO

The Cotillion Room is bustling with preparations for the revival of the Snow Ball. Someone is setting up tables, LUCY and others are on stepladders in work clothes, stringing up a large sign: "WELCOME BACK, KITTY AND JACK!" Downstage, COOPER addresses the audience:

COOPER: . . . And so the day arrived. There were articles in the paper, interviews on TV, and a special exhibit at the Historical Society with pictures of Jack and Kitty, and taped interviews of people who had seen them dance. . . .

(BREWSTER, *who has been working on the decorations, calls to* BILLY.)

BREWSTER: Question for a fellow sports fan.

BILLY: Yo.

BREWSTER: How many times did Jack and Kitty dance during their final season together?

BILLY: Are we talking home, or away?

BREWSTER: Both, naturally.

BILLY: Twenty-seven times, according to the latest statistics.

BREWSTER: Wrong. Twenty-nine. They danced twice in Toronto.

BILLY: Canada? We're counting Canada now? Since when do we count Canada?

COOPER (*to audience*): We became the hottest ticket in town. . . .

(SAUL *comes up to him.*)

SAUL: Hey, Coop, can you do me a favor? I need two tickets tonight for me and Rhoda.

COOPER: We're sold out, pal. Sorry.

SAUL: Couldn't you squeeze us in? I'll pay for it. Extra.

COOPER: Tell you what, Saul. We're setting up bleachers in back. Give your name to Mrs. Klinger.

SAUL: Bleachers? For Rhoda? You must be mad.

COOPER: Or . . .

SAUL: Or what?

COOPER: You could help underwrite a sponsor's table.

SAUL: That's blackmail, Coop. But I'll call you.

(*He goes out.*)

COOPER (*to audience*): I wish I could say the day dawned bright and clear. But it didn't. It dawned damp and gray. And we all knew, without knowing we knew, that we were in for a major snowstorm . . .

(LIZ *comes on in parka and boots, carrying* COOPER*'s tuxedo in a plastic bag.*)

LIZ: Here's your stuff, Cooper. Tux, shirt, studs, everything.

COOPER: Thanks. I'll change in the men's room.

LIZ: That tuxedo cost a small fortune to repair, by the way. It was riddled with moth holes.

COOPER: Just as long as it fits.

LIZ: It never did, remember?

COOPER: What's it like outside?

LIZ: Beginning to snow. I wonder if they'll make it.

COOPER: They'll make it. What's a little snow between friends?

LIZ: See you later, then.

(*She starts off, then stops, calls up to* LUCY, *who's still on ladder.*)

Hey, is that sign fireproof?

LUCY: Of course, Liz.

LIZ: Are you sure? These manufacturers get away with murder these days.

COOPER: It's okay, Liz.

LIZ: Well, I'm worried about people who smoke. I think you should rope them off, at the far end of the room.

LUCY: We're not going to do that, Liz.

COOPER: It's okay, Lucy.

LUCY: Anyway, why do you care, Liz? I hear you have another party on your agenda tonight.

LIZ: Right. Over at the Community Center. (*Rhythmically:*)
Tell Jack and Kitty to forget this fuss,
For some free-style rap dancing over with us.

(*She executes a step and goes out.*)

LUCY (*coming down off the ladder*): She hates me, doesn't she?

COOPER: Naw.

LUCY: She wouldn't look at me.

COOPER: She's got a lot on her mind.

LUCY: She's got *us* on her mind.

COOPER: I wish she did.

LUCY: What does that mean?

COOPER: Skip it.

LUCY: Tell her, Cooper.

COOPER: Tell her what?

LUCY: Everything. That we love each other, and want to get married.

COOPER: I will.

LUCY: You keep saying that, but you don't.

COOPER: I'm waiting for the right time.

LUCY: Tell her tonight.

COOPER: Tonight?

LUCY: After the Snow Ball. To clear the air.

COOPER: I can't just take my wife home after a festive occasion and tell her I'm leaving.

LUCY: Cooper, I am out on a limb here! I just got fired because of this goddamn "festive occasion"!

COOPER: What?

LUCY: They noticed the telephone bill . . . all those long-distance calls to Kitty.

COOPER: Oh, boy.

LUCY: Oh, well. I can still call Minneapolis.

COOPER: Hey, look . . .

LUCY: I'm serious, Cooper. Tonight's the night. Now bite the bullet. Or get off the pot.

(*She goes out.*)

COOPER (*to audience*): Oh, God! Can a man be in love with two women at the same time? Which way do I turn? Lucy, with her satin nightgowns, and agreeable ways, and spectacular behavior in bed—oh, Lucy, I'm young again when I'm with you! She's found this cozy little carriage house off in the woods, and is already thumbing through the Laura Ashley catalogue. Why shouldn't I settle there, and listen to good old songs, and read good old books, and watch "Masterpiece Theatre" on Sunday nights? What's wrong with that? . . . Of course, there's Liz. Impossible Liz. Fighting her past, fighting the world, fighting *me*, all the way to the finish. Only after we're dead will I get off the hook. Then I can relax. In hell, with all the other adulterers. While Liz goes straight to heaven. Of course, once she's there, I'm sure she'll spend most of her time getting God to register as a Democrat.

(*A* MUSICIAN *comes up to* COOPER; *he carries a clarinet.*)

MUSICIAN: Mr. Jones, we're ready to rehearse in the back room.

COOPER (*getting a stack of music; to* MUSICIAN): Could you start by running through these arrangements? Because of the snow, the dancers might be a little late.

MUSICIAN (*looking them over*): Hey, this is great stuff! Where'd you dig it up?

COOPER: It's a long story. . . .

MUSICIAN: I think the boys will get a kick out of these. . . .

(*He goes off.* JACK *appears, carrying an identical stack of musical arrangements. He wears informal clothes: a sweater, gray flannels, white bucks.*)

JACK (*as if on telephone*): Coop, I got to talk to you. Can you meet me at Smithers'?

(MR. SMITHERS *begins to set up the drugstore counter.*)

COOPER: I'll be there.

(COOPER *and* JACK *meet at the counter.*)

JACK (*tossing* COOPER *the arrangements*): Here's a souvenir for you.

COOPER: What's this?

JACK: Our music. Take it. It's worth over three hundred bucks.

COOPER: Hey, simmer down. What's the matter?

JACK: We're breaking up.

COOPER: You and Kitty?

JACK: Her parents are packing her off to Europe. They won't even let her go back for the second semester. Off she goes, the day after tomorrow.

COOPER: Why?

JACK: Because of that goddamn Snow Ball.

COOPER: You were spectacular at the Snow Ball.

JACK: Tell that to her parents. They thought it was vulgar.

COOPER: Vulgar?

JACK: That's what her mother said. Cheap and vulgar. Hollywood stuff. That's what she said.

COOPER: Oh, for chrissake!

JACK: And it didn't help when this *agent* called. From New York.

COOPER: A New York agent!

JACK: He saw us in Boston, and saw us again here, and offered us two hundred and fifty dollars a week, each, plus expenses, to work at a nightclub in Toledo!

COOPER: That's a lot of dough!

JACK: And we'd get second billing. We'd go on right after Henny Youngman!

COOPER: Oh, hey, wow!

JACK: I know. Just think. Dance with Kitty eight times a week, and get *paid* for it!

COOPER: Did Kitty go along with it?

JACK: Sure! She was raring to go! Hell, maybe we would have ended up in the movies!

COOPER: You still could, Jack.

JACK: That's what her folks were scared of. So they lowered the boom. We all had this big scene. Her mother starts to scream, Kitty starts to cry, the old man kicks me out of the house. Then Kitty calls today and says she's off to Europe.

COOPER: I thought her father liked you.

JACK: He did, until the Snow Ball. Now he thinks I'm just an Irishman on the make.

COOPER: Well, you are a little, Jack.

JACK: I know I am. But that's not all I am.

COOPER: She'll be back, Jack.

JACK: That's what she says. But it'll be too *late*, Coop! I *know* her! She's lazy. Some guy will give her a big rush, and I won't be there to dance her out of it.

(*Upstage, on the opposite side,* KITTY *comes out in a wedding dress, carrying two glasses of champagne, being congratulated by well-wishers.*)

So here: take the music. They can play it when you marry Liz.

COOPER (*taking the arrangements*): I'll keep it for you, Jack. You'll be dancing with Kitty again, I swear.

JACK: Oh, Coop. Grow up! You're just a dreamer, like everyone else around here!

(JACK *goes off as* KITTY *calls to* COOPER *from across the stage. There is dance music in the background.*)

KITTY: Cooper!

(COOPER *crosses to her.*)

You haven't kissed the bride yet.

(COOPER *gives her a perfunctory kiss.*)

Oh, Cooper, don't be mad. Please. He's a wonderful guy.

COOPER: He's not Jack.

KITTY: He's more my *type*, Cooper. Really. His family knows my family, and he skis like a dream. We had the most fabulous time in Switzerland.

COOPER: Does he dance?

KITTY (*defiantly*): Yes. Very well. He dances very well.

COOPER: I saw you dance with him out there. He could hardly move.

KITTY: That's because he hurt his ankle.

COOPER: Oh, Kitty.

KITTY: He has a bad *ankle*, Cooper. From lacrosse. At Princeton.

COOPER: Bullshit, Kitty. That's bullshit, and you know it.

KITTY: Oh, stop, Cooper. Please. Just stop.

COOPER: Jack's here, by the way.

KITTY: I know that. Why wouldn't I know that? I invited him. We've had a long talk. Everything's fine. He's got a scholarship for law school, and made big plans.

COOPER: I notice you wouldn't dance with him.

KITTY: I don't know what you mean.

COOPER: I saw him cut in on you, and you sat right down.

KITTY: I was tired, Cooper.

COOPER: You were scared, Kitty.

KITTY: That's ridiculous.

COOPER: You were scared he'd dance you right out the door!

KITTY (*starting to cry*): Don't, Cooper. Please. I can't stand it.

COOPER (*touching her*): Why'd you do it, Kitty?

KITTY: There's more to life than hanging around nightclubs.

COOPER: That's your mother talking.

KITTY: There's more to life than dancing, then.

COOPER: You were lazy, Kitty. You made a lazy choice. It was just easier to slide downhill.

KITTY: You can't always marry the perfect person, Cooper! No one does!

COOPER: You can try.

KITTY: Anyway, Jack's *found* someone, Cooper! He says he's almost *engaged*! He says she types his papers, and is terribly well organized, and will be a big help in his career.

(*The sounds of an airport.* JOAN DALEY *appears. She is neat and well dressed. She looks around impatiently.*)

She'll be much better for him than I'd ever be!

(KITTY *runs off in tears, as a* WAITRESS *sets up a cocktail table.* LUCY *joins* COOPER, *indicates* JOAN.)

LUCY: She must be the one.

(*They cross to* JOAN.)

JOAN: Oh, hi. I'm terribly sorry to drag you two all the way out to the airport, but I was between planes, and I thought I'd just give you a jingle. I'm Joan Daley.

COOPER: Hiya.

LUCY: Hello.

(*Everyone shakes hands. They settle at the table.* JOAN *gestures imperiously to the* WAITRESS.)

JOAN: I just spent the weekend at Andover visiting the boys, and I have to be back for a major fund-raiser in Indianapolis tonight, but I thought I ought to stop by and say hello. (*She briskly removes her gloves.*) And, frankly, I thought we should lay our cards on the table. Before this Snow Ball thing gets completely out of hand.

LUCY: Out of hand?

JOAN (*to* WAITRESS): Piña colada, please.

LUCY: White wine.

COOPER: Light beer.

(*The* WAITRESS *goes off angrily.*)

JOAN (*pulling a pack of cigarettes out of her purse; looking around*): Do you suppose Jack will lose the election if I sneak one tiny little menthol light? I mean, wives have to be so careful in politics. . . .

(*She offers them to* COOPER *and* LUCY, *who shake their heads.*)

No? How disgustingly healthy. (*She lights up and takes a deep draw.*) Well. Tell me. How serious is it? This . . . Snow Ball?

COOPER: Sort of serious.

LUCY: Very serious.

JOAN: You mean you seriously want Jack to *dance*? My Jack? Republican candidate for governor Jack Daley? You want him to dance around some room with some old flame?

LUCY: That's what we want.

JOAN: The kids think it's an absolute hoot. We all roared about it when he told us.

COOPER: Jack was a great dancer.

JOAN: So he says. He's out in the garage, every chance he gets, practicing to some tape. I mean, who are we kidding?

LUCY: You're in for a big surprise.

JOAN: Let's be a tad more specific. Will the media be there? Photographers? Television? Any of that?

COOPER: Oh, sure. It's a story, after all. Downtown renewal, the hotel fixed up . . .

JOAN: So it will be on TV.

COOPER: Local TV, certainly.

JOAN: *Our* TV, too, I should think. Candidate returns to roots, all that . . .

LUCY: Actually, there's talk of *national* TV. "Entertainment Tonight" has made some inquiries.

JOAN: Don't count on it, folks.

LUCY: Well, I mean, it's a story, after all. Two old friends come home to dance . . .

JOAN: It's a local story, here and back home.

COOPER: Probably. Yes.

JOAN: Suppose *I* danced with him.

COOPER: I hope you will.

JOAN: No, I mean instead of her.

LUCY: Mrs. Daley . . .

JOAN: Joan.

LUCY: All right, Joan.

JOAN: Actually, we *have* danced a little. We've—we've done the twist. We were—quite good.

COOPER: Well, you can dance the twist again, if you'd like, Mrs. Daley.

JOAN: Joan.

COOPER: We're hoping, Joan, that Jack will dance the main dance with Kitty.

JOAN: I'm the main dance, mister.

LUCY: Well, we know you are, but—

JOAN: I'm his *wife*.

LUCY: Oh, well . . .

JOAN: He can dance, okay. He can even do a number, off camera, with this Kitty. But when it comes to magic time, he dances with me.

COOPER: It's just for old times' sake. . . .

LUCY: Exactly. It's just a fun thing.

JOAN: Just a fun thing? You tell that to the unemployed steelworkers in Gary watching it on TV. You tell that to the farmers downstate up to their ass in debt. You tell that to me, *me*, who shook all those sweaty hands and sat through all those lousy speeches for twenty years. Just a fun thing! You think

I'm going to sit on the sidelines and watch my husband throw
away a chance to be governor, just so he can bounce around
with some society broad? No sirree, gang. Sorry. He dances
with me or he doesn't dance at all.

COOPER: Does Jack go along with that?

JOAN: He better. (*She puts on her gloves.*) Otherwise I won't come
with him. Which will look bad. And I might not be there
when he gets back. Which will look worse. Now where the
fuck is the ladies' room? (*She gets up.*)

LUCY: I think it's—

JOAN (*extending her hand*): Thank you very much. What a lovely
city. What a lovely airport. What a pleasant way to break up
my trip.

(*She goes out.*)

LUCY (*to* COOPER): Maybe I can still butter her up.

COOPER: I'm amazed she got through security.

(LUCY *hurries off after* JOAN.)

LUCY: Wait, Mrs. Daley . . . Joan . . . Wait . . .

(*Meanwhile, on the opposite side of the stage,* BALDWIN HALL, *a
tanned, white-haired, elderly man in resort clothes, has come on with a
telephone.*)

BALDWIN (*on telephone*): Cooper Jones?

COOPER (*as if on the telephone*): Who's this?

BALDWIN: It's Baldwin Hall. Kitty's husband.

COOPER: Ah.

BALDWIN: I wonder if I might talk to you about this Snow Ball business.

COOPER: Shoot.

BALDWIN (*putting on a jacket and tie*): I prefer it to be face-to-face. My plane gets in at four-forty-five.

COOPER: I'll be there.

(*A white-jacketed* WAITER *sets up a table and chairs.* COOPER *and* BALDWIN *meet center, and shake hands.*)

I thought we'd go to the club.

BALDWIN: Any place where it's quiet.

(*They cross to the table and order from the* WAITER *as they settle in.*)

I'll have a gin martini on the rocks with a twist, please.

COOPER: Light beer, Martin.

BALDWIN (*looking around*): Nice club. Did Kitty ever dance here?

COOPER: Every spring. In the courtyard.

BALDWIN: She's a lovely dancer.

COOPER: I'll say.

BALDWIN: Even with an old fool like me. We dance very well together. Every Thursday night we go to the golf club down at Ocean Reef and dance under the stars.

COOPER: Sounds great.

(*The* WAITER *brings drinks.*)

BALDWIN: Well. Now. This Snow Ball thing. How definite is it?

COOPER: Pretty definite.

BALDWIN: Sometimes these things don't materialize.

COOPER: The invitations are out. The band's all signed up.

BALDWIN: Then the die is cast.

COOPER: I'm afraid it is. Some problem?

BALDWIN (*drinking*): Kitty's not very well. . . . Actually, she's . . . in serious difficulty. She's got . . . During the operation, they discovered . . . They say I could lose her. (*He starts to cry.*)

COOPER: Oh, hey, please. Would you like to go somewhere? We have a lounge here. We have a library which is never used. . . .

BALDWIN (*shaking his head*): I'm all right. I'm fine now. (*He taps his glass.*) I'd like another of these, if I may. (COOPER *signals the* WAITER.) She refuses to do anything about it until after the party. She's heard you can lose your hair. . . .

COOPER: Boy. (*To* WAITER:) More of the same for Mr. Hall, Martin. And I might shift to scotch.

BALDWIN: She wants to risk her life, come up here in the dead of winter, dance with some fellow she hasn't seen for thirty years. I can't get over it. I can't make it out.

(*The* WAITER *brings more drinks.*)

COOPER: Do you want me to find some way to call it off?

BALDWIN: She'd never forgive me.

COOPER: Well, then, look. All she needs to do is a few steps, really. Just a bow and a spin. Then we'll put her right back on the plane.

BALDWIN: No. She wants to do the whole thing. She took the music you sent her, and found some fella who plays the piano, and she's been working on her steps ever since. She's very serious about it.

COOPER: Oh, boy.

BALDWIN: This man. Jack Daley. Is he serious, too?

COOPER: I think he is.

BALDWIN: Is he practicing, too?

COOPER: I hear he is.

BALDWIN: Good. Because she wants this to work. It's terribly important to her. (*He downs his drink, gets up.*) And therefore to me. Now, if you'll return me to the airport . . .

COOPER: Won't you have some dinner?

BALDWIN: No thank you. I can just get back for a late supper with Kitty.

COOPER: Tell her I hope she feels better.

BALDWIN: I'll tell her nothing at all. She thinks I'm playing golf in Fort Lauderdale.

COOPER: I'll tell Jack to go easy.

BALDWIN: Sir: we have just had a drink at your club. I assume everything we discussed was strictly confidential. You may simply tell him to dance as well as he possibly can.

(*He goes off as the* WAITER *clears the table.*)

    (*The lights come up on the Cotillion Room, now all prepared and decorated for the Snow Ball.* LUCY *comes on, carrying some decoration.*)

LUCY: Cooper! We just heard on the radio. The storm's worse. The airport has closed down.

COOPER: Oh, God.

LUCY: I called the airlines. Jack's plane never took off, and Kitty's stacked up somewhere over Albany.

COOPER: Shit.

LUCY: So what do we do?

COOPER: Do? We do what we always do in times of trouble: we change our clothes.

(*He goes off.*)

LUCY (*calling after him*): And then we change our *lives*, Cooper Jones!

(*No answer.* LUCY *throws up her hands, goes off another way.*)

    (*Music. Lights. Decorations drop into place. Guests enter down the staircase in their evening clothes and overcoats; among them are* SAUL *and* RHODA RADNER.)

CALVIN (*brushing off his shoulders*): God! What weather!

MARY: Who cares? Look at this!

RHODA: Let it snow, let it snow, let it snow!

A MAN: Dig the music!

RHODA: It's like walking into the Piazza San Marco when the band strikes up!

SAUL: Rhoda never got over our trip to Venice.

HEATHER: Let's hope those Arthur Murray brushups pay off!

(*She starts a tentative tango with* BREWSTER.)

CALVIN (*to his wife,* MARY): What say, Mary? Think we can still cut a rug?

MARY: Go easy, Calvin. I've had a hip replacement.

SAUL: Look at the floor, Rhoda. Notice the workmanship!

RHODA: They should've gotten Johnson's Wax to underwrite this thing. (*Looking at the tango dancers:*) Olé!

(*Downstage,* OLDER JACK *enters, in an overcoat. He carries a Val-Pac bag over his shoulder. He is ruddy faced, gray haired, and looks at least fifty. He watches the dancing for a moment, then speaks to a* WAITER.)

OLDER JACK: Would you find Mr. Cooper Jones, and tell him I'm here?

WAITER: Who shall I say it is, sir?

OLDER JACK: He'll know.

(*The* WAITER *goes off.* JACK *looks around.*)

BREWSTER (*To* HEATHER *as they tango*): My grandmother danced on this floor!

HEATHER: We should've brought her! We should've dragged her out of that nursing home!

RHODA (*removing her coat*): Oh, but the lights, the music! I feel like Madame Bovary!

SAUL: Just don't act like Madame Bovary!

(COOPER *comes out, now in his tuxedo.*)

COOPER (*to* JACK): May I help you?

JACK: I certainly hope so.

COOPER (*peering at him*): Jack?

JACK (*holding out his hand*): Hiya, guy.

COOPER: Jack! My God. Jack . . .

(*They embrace.*)

You look . . . great, Jack.

JACK: I look old, Coop. And so do you. (*Indicating the others.*) So does everyone. It's been thirty years.

COOPER (*looking at the others*): Right. I never noticed. . . . But hey! How did you get here? Your flight was canceled.

JACK: I took an earlier one.

COOPER: I would've met you, Jack.

JACK: Naaa. I needed to get my bearings. Things sure have changed, haven't they? Smithers' is now a video store.

COOPER: Right. But hey, but you're here! (*He calls toward the dancers.*) Hey, gang! Look who's—

JACK (*shushing him*): Hold it. Where is she?

COOPER: Hasn't shown up yet.

JACK: Knew it! She chickened out, didn't she?

COOPER: The *storm*, Jack. Remember?

JACK: Oh. Right.

COOPER: Let's hope she's just . . . late.

JACK (*nervously laughing*): Where have we heard that one before?

(*The other guests have drifted out.*)

COOPER: We never thought we'd get through to you, Jack! All those letters, those telephone calls! But here you are! And you get the VIP treatment, buddy. We're giving you the Executive Suite, free of charge, with a telephone in the john!

JACK: Thanks, but I'll stay with my mother.

COOPER (*carefully*): Your wife isn't with you?

JACK: She . . . couldn't make it.

COOPER: That's too bad.

JACK: Yes. That is. That is too bad. Well. I better get into my monkey suit, huh?

COOPER: Come on. You can still use the suite for that.

(*They go off. Police sirens.* BALDWIN *comes on with* LUCY; *both are in evening clothes.*)

BALDWIN: Well, we're here. And it's been hell getting here. And I'm not sure why we're here. But we're here.

LUCY: I'm sorry, but I'm hopelessly confused. Where is Kitty?

BALDWIN: Getting dressed, of course. I engaged a room.

LUCY: But what were those sirens? And who were all those policemen?

BALDWIN: It's very simple, really. We had to land in Syracuse, so Kitty insisted on renting a car. And insisted on driving at an unconscionable speed. Naturally she plowed into a snow-bank. The troopers dug us out, and Kitty charmed her way into a police escort right to the front door.

LUCY: The gods are with us!

BALDWIN: Then do you suppose the gods could provide us with a good, stiff drink?

LUCY (*taking his arm*): That you shall have, sir. That you shall have.

(*They go off. More music.* LIZ *comes on, in an overcoat. She looks around.* COOPER *comes on.*)

COOPER: Well, well. You're early.

LIZ: The kids wanted the car. They dropped me off.

COOPER: Aren't they coming? I reserved them seats in the bleachers.

LIZ: They decided on the movies instead.

COOPER: Son of a *bitch*!

LIZ: They said you and I don't show up for the Grateful Dead —why should they for Jack and Kitty?

COOPER: You should have made them stay.

LIZ: We can't *make* them do things anymore, Cooper. They're too old. And so are we.

COOPER: Let me take your coat. (*He takes off Liz's coat.*) Hey! (*She's wearing a lovely green dress.*)

LIZ: What's the matter?

COOPER: The green dress from Berger's.

LIZ: They had it on sale.

COOPER: You look good.

LIZ: I don't know . . .

COOPER: You look gorgeous.

LIZ: I must say, getting into these duds gets all the old juices going.

COOPER: What did I tell you? (*He starts dancing with her.*)

LIZ (*as they dance*): Smell the perfume?

COOPER: Do I ever. What's it called?

LIZ: Some dumb name. I borrowed it from Mother.

COOPER (*stopping dancing*): Liz, before the preliminaries, I want to ask you something important.

LIZ: Ask away.

COOPER: Are you happy?

LIZ: Happy?

COOPER: Here. With me. Tonight.

LIZ: You want me to speak frankly?

COOPER: Yes I do, Liz. I really do.

LIZ: All right then, Cooper. Yes and no.

COOPER: Give me the yes first.

LIZ: Okay. Yes, I like getting gussied up occasionally. I like being with you, dressed or undressed. I even like it when we fight. We keep each other honest, and I like that a lot. So yes, yes, yes, to all of that.

COOPER: And now the no.

LIZ: I don't think you've thought about the morning after.

COOPER: Which means . . . ?

LIZ: Which means that after every party, somebody has to clean up the crap.

COOPER: Watch your language, lady.

LIZ: This is no lady. This is your wife.

(LUCY, BALDWIN, *and the others come on.*)

BALDWIN: There is much to be said for a good drink with good company when you're a poor traveler on a snowy night.

COOPER (*handing champagne around*): Anybody need champagne?

LUCY: Notice the decorations, everyone. We're having the champagne cooled in real snow.

(OLDER JACK *comes in, now resplendent in tails.*)

COOPER: Aha! Here he is. Jack, let me introduce you to—

JACK (*arm around* BALDWIN): That's all right. We met in the corridor, didn't we, Baldwin?

BALDWIN: We did indeed. And cemented our friendship in the bar.

LUCY (*low, to* COOPER): They seem to get along.

COOPER: They seem to like each other.

BALDWIN (*raising his glass; pointedly*): Ladies and gentlemen, I would like to propose a toast. To Kitty.

JACK: To Kitty.

COOPER: To all of us.

LIZ: To a better world.

LUCY (*low, to* COOPER): To you and me, tomorrow.

(COOPER *winces.*)

JACK: Still no Kitty?

EVERYONE ELSE: She's getting dressed, Jack.

LUCY: For a while we thought we'd lost her.

LIZ: Oh, well, then you could have gone on in her place.

LUCY: What kind of a fool do you think I am?

LIZ: I've never been quite sure.

LUCY (*grabbing* COOPER *by the arm*): Did you hear that? I'm going to tell her myself!

COOPER: Lucy—

(*A TV crew enters. A woman* INTERVIEWER *speaks into a recorder.*)

INTERVIEWER: We are now coming into the Cotillion Room of the old George Washington Hotel, as guests gather to celebrate the homecoming of two special friends. . . . (*She finds*

JACK, *shoves a microphone in his face*.) Mr. Daley: How does it feel to come home and dance with an old flame?

JACK: I think you'd do better to call us young sparks. . . . Is there an ambulance waiting in the wings?

(*Laughter from the group.*)

INTERVIEWER: As a candidate for governor, are you concerned about the lack of any minority representation at this party?

JACK: Oh, these folks are a minority. They just don't know it yet.

(*Laughter from crowd.*)

COOPER (*low, to* OLDER JACK): I see you're still light on your feet, Jack.

INTERVIEWER: It's hard to believe you'd remember all your old steps.

JACK: I've got a memory like an elephant. I'll probably dance like one, too.

(*More laughter. The crowd moves upstage for more interviews, as* COOPER *steps forward*.)

COOPER (*to audience*): "What have I done?" says Alec Guinness, as he surveys the bridge over the River Kwai. What in God's name have I done? Why are we here in this tacky old room? Everyone's trying much too hard, and no one's having a good time. Jack is obviously in bad trouble at home, and seems to have been drinking since noon. Poor Kitty is probably crumped out on some couch. And me? What about me? My job is in shambles—I haven't sold anything in weeks. I've had to borrow money, just to buy Christmas presents. And my marriage? Have I messed it up permanently? Is Liz thinking about divorce? Will I end up with Lucy, living on sex and nostalgia? Oh, what have I done, Guinness asks himself, before he throws himself on the plunger and blows the whole damn thing to smithereens!

(*A cry of delight from the staircase. Everyone looks toward it in anticipation.*)

And then Kitty arrived and it all made perfect sense!

(*The* OLDER KITTY *enters as she once entered in dancing school. She wears a lovely dress, but like* JACK, *she is now much older.*)

KITTY: Oops! I guess I'm late.

(*Applause from the crowd. The television camera moves in, and the television lights come on. She blinks.*)

What do I do now? Say "cheese," or what?

BALDWIN (*going to her*): You're home, darling.

(*He helps her with her coat, gives her his arm, and walks her downstairs. Squeals and hugs as she greets her old friends. Finally* BALDWIN *brings her through the crowd to* JACK. *More applause.* JACK *bows to* KITTY, *as if it were the old days.*)

KITTY: Oh, well, why not? Let's do it from soup to nuts.

(*She responds with a deep curtsy. Applause again from the crowd. They kiss.*)

JACK: You look great, Kitty.

KITTY: I feel like an old Studebaker, trotted out for an antique show.

JACK: No, no. You look terrific.

KITTY: Thank you, Jack. So do you.

MARY: Come on, you two! Dance!

LUCY: But everyone's not here yet.

BALDWIN: It might be good to get started.

KITTY (*to* JACK): Do you suppose we could sneak out and practice a little?

(*The crowd calls out:* "No! No! Do it now!")

Hey, come on! Give us a break.

JACK: Looks like there isn't time, Kitty. We'll just have to hope for the best.

KITTY: I tried going through it on my own. Some of it came back, some of it didn't.

JACK: Ditto with me. It's hard to dance alone.

KITTY: At least tell the band to go slow. Say we're no spring chickens.

JACK: You're young as a girl.

KITTY: Still. Tell them.

(JACK *goes off;* KITTY *glances around.*)

Cooper Jones, is that you? Where have you been hiding? Crawl from there, you bad boy! You should be ashamed of yourself, putting me on the spot this way.

COOPER (*coming to her*): Oh, Kitty, you'll come through with flying colors.

(*They hug.*)

KITTY: Well, flying or not, get me a glass of water, and all will be forgiven.

(BALDWIN *brings her a pill;* COOPER *produces a glass of water.* KITTY *downs the pill quickly, and smiles.*)

COOPER: Are you all right?

KITTY: Fine. Never better.

LUCY: Surprise, surprise!

(*Out comes the old Snow Ball sleigh, drawn by two men.*)

Prance, gentlemen, prance!

EVERYONE: You're supposed to be reindeer!

KITTY: Where'd you find that? In the ruins of Pompeii?

COOPER (*leading* KITTY *to it*): Sit in it, Kitty. . . . And Lucy . . . and Liz, sit beside her.

LIZ: You're not going to get me into that thing!

COOPER: Do it, Liz. Please. Once, without arguing.

LIZ: All right. But under protest.

(LIZ *joins* KITTY *and* LUCY *in the sleigh. The TV people focus in. Everyone applauds, then freezes.*)

COOPER (*to audience*): Oh, my God, you see? You see? This is it! This is what I've wanted all along! Woman, in all her glory! (*Indicating* KITTY:) Goddess . . . (*Indicating* LIZ:) Wife and mother . . . (*Indicating* LUCY:) And finally, lover! Oh, if I could only have all three forever!

LIZ: Cooper, you're in the way! (*The freeze breaks.*)

JACK (*returning*): The orchestra's all set. (*He sees* KITTY *and her court, stands enrapt.*) Holy cow.

KITTY: Let's get at it. I think I'm sitting on a nail.

(JACK *lifts her out of the sleigh, as before.* LUCY *tells others to remove it, shoos the TV people out of the way.* JACK *and* KITTY *assume their old starting position.*)

Well, then. It's all a question of faith, isn't it? I mean, we'll just have to hold our noses and jump.

JACK: That's it.

(*The crowd backs off, settles into chairs or stands along the wall.* JACK *signals. The orchestra sounds a drumroll.*)

KITTY (*holding up her hand*): Hold it.

(*The drumroll stops.*)

I don't know . . . Jack and I have come so far . . . and all these people have managed to brave the storm. . . . Shouldn't we join hands and pray, or sing "The Star-Spangled Banner," or something?

(General laughter.)

    (Then the number begins. JACK *and* KITTY *dance their old Snow Ball number, to the same music, but because they're older now, and out of shape, and out of practice, they make many mistakes. Some of it works beautifully, and the crowd supports them with "ooh"s and "ah"s and occasional applause. As the dancers continue, the* YOUNG JACK *and* KITTY *join them, swirling and dipping around them, until soon we are seeing the number from several simultaneous perspectives—a complicated, intricate, shifting quartet, sometimes gloriously nostalgic, sometimes precariously out of date. Finally, as the music moves to its conclusion, the younger couple disappears, and the* OLDER JACK *and* KITTY *manage a good enough finish to bring on a round of decent applause. At the end, people cluster around them, congratulating them. Others begin to drift off.)*

MARY *(to* HEATHER*)*: How can you leave after seeing something like that? They make me want to dance all night!

HEATHER: I have to baby-sit tomorrow for our grandchildren.

(She goes off.)

CALVIN: Well, we've seen it. Now I can die happily.

MARY: Oh, Calvin . . .

CALVIN: No, I mean it. I've seen the Parthenon, I've seen the Taj Mahal, I've seen Jack and Kitty. It's all downhill from here.

MARY: Can't we at least take a peek at the Grand Canyon?

(They go off. COOPER, LIZ, *and* LUCY *are in the crowd of well-wishers.)*

COOPER: Champagne for Jack and Kitty!

(*Cheers.*)

KITTY: No thank you, Cooper. (*She glances at* BALDWIN.) I think it's time I was in bed.

BALDWIN: I agree.

(*He slips her another pill, which she swallows surreptitiously.*)

LUCY: Now you and Baldwin are staying with me, Kitty.

KITTY: We can't, Lucy. We decided to stay right here in this hotel. That way we can be off bright and early.

BALDWIN: The policeman said the airport would be clear tomorrow.

KITTY: Yes, all this snow is supposed just to melt away.

LUCY: But we have a luncheon planned. And a tour of all the old sights.

KITTY: Don't dare, love. I'd probably never leave.

(*She starts kissing people goodbye, as* BALDWIN *follows her, shaking hands.*)

Goodbye, goodbye. . . . Lovely to see you again. . . . Hey, don't everybody stop dancing! Goodbye. . . . Such fun. . . . Come to Florida. . . . Come see us. . . . Goodbye.

(COOPER *and* LUCY *accompany them towards an exit.* KITTY *turns to them.*)

So long, you two. Thank you for asking me back. (*She kisses* LUCY, *then* COOPER.)

COOPER: Kitty, you were great.

KITTY: Well, at least it ties things up, Cooper. I had to do that.

JACK (*agonizingly*): Kitty!

KITTY: Did you think I'd forget you? Come here, you sweet man, so I can say a special goodbye.

JACK: We did okay, didn't we, Kitty?

KITTY: Well, we tried our damnedest.

JACK: We could try again.

KITTY: Oh, Jack . . .

JACK: I mean, just dancing occasionally.

KITTY: Wouldn't that be fun?

JACK: I could visit in Florida. Or you could—

KITTY: Oh, heavens no, Jack. As Shakespeare says . . . (*She gives him a quick kiss on the cheek.*) Enough is enough.

BALDWIN (*taking her arm*): Come on, dear.

KITTY: Goodbye, Jack darling. And thank you.

JACK: Goodbye, Kitty.

(KITTY *and* BALDWIN *go. More people also leave.*)

COOPER: Champagne, Jack?

JACK (*looking after* KITTY): What? . . . Oh, no thanks.

COOPER: Scotch, then? Something. We haven't really caught up.

JACK: Actually, Coop, now I'm back, I'd better go all the way. The clarinet player is an old pal from Holy Angels. He wants to go out and hoist a few brews.

COOPER: I'll pick you up tomorrow, then. Show you around.

JACK: No thanks, friend. It's breakfast with me dear old mum, then off to face the music.

COOPER: The campaign?

JACK: No, no. Actually, there won't be a campaign this year, Coop. Marriage troubles. Things are kind of messy.

COOPER: Oh, Jack, I'm sorry.

JACK: Naaa. Would've happened anyway. This just brought things to a boil.

COOPER: Then come home, Jack. Work here. Run for office if you want. I'll help. Look, I feel responsible. I stirred this up.

JACK: I'm glad you did, buddy. (*He looks toward where* KITTY *has gone.*) It was worth it, even after thirty years. (*Pause.*) Well. Onward and upward.

COOPER: So what's next, Jack?

JACK: You know me. I guess I'll land on my feet. (*He does his old dance step from dancing school.*)

COOPER: I'm sure you will, Jack.

JACK: So long then, pal.

(*They hug, and he goes off.* SAUL *comes in, now in his overcoat.*)

SAUL: Rhoda's in the car, Coop. She overdid the champagne.

COOPER: I'm sorry, Saul.

SAUL: But I wanted to say thanks. It reminded me of those dances we saw on our cruise to the South Pacific. I mean, it told some story, even if we didn't know what it was.

COOPER: Thanks, Saul.

SAUL: Call me Monday. We'll talk business.

COOPER: Maybe, Saul. Thanks.

(SAUL *goes off. The TV crew is packing up.* LUCY *sits down forlornly at one of the tables.* LIZ *comes up to* COOPER.)

LIZ: I'll change for the community shindig.

COOPER: I'd better do a little cleaning up.

LIZ (*glancing at* LUCY): Yes. You'd better.

(LIZ *goes off.* COOPER *takes off his jacket, crosses to* LUCY. *Others continue to drift off.*)

COOPER: The snow's stopping.

LUCY: I know. . . . (*Pause.*) I didn't tell you this, but I was asked out to Minneapolis for New Year's. (*Looks at him.*) Think I should go?

COOPER: I think you should.

LUCY: I think I should, too. (*Getting up:*) He's very different, you know. He was born in *Bulgaria,* for God's sake. He sells wall-to-wall carpeting, and wants me to help him in his work. It'll be a whole new thing.

COOPER: Maybe that's good.

LUCY: Maybe it is. . . . I wonder what we thought we were doing.

COOPER: Putting a little romance back into the world.

LUCY: Oh, is that what it was?

COOPER: I thought they were spectacular!

LUCY (*kissing him on the cheek*): Oh, Cooper! You're more romantic than any of us!

(*She goes out. He watches her go. The lights dim on the room. The* INTERVIEWER *and* CAMERAMAN *are puttering with their equipment.*)

COOPER: Did you get it, people?

CAMERAMAN: What's to get? Some fat guy pushing an old broad around the room.

COOPER: I don't believe I heard you correctly.

CAMERAMAN: Hey. You get better dancing every day on MTV.

COOPER: You have no idea what you're talking about.

CAMERAMAN: You speaking to me, buddy?

INTERVIEWER: Let's split, Eddie. Okay?

COOPER (*coming up to the* CAMERAMAN): I'll tell you what you saw tonight. You saw a class act. You saw a man and a woman dance beautifully together. You saw the man lead and the woman follow—no, that's wrong, you saw her *choose* to follow, of her own accord. You saw grace and charm and harmony between the sexes. You saw an image of civilization up there tonight, that's what you fucking well saw! (*He shoves the* CAMERAMAN.)

CAMERAMAN: Want to make something of it, buddy?

INTERVIEWER: Forget it, Eddie. He's drunk.

COOPER: Sure I want to make something of it.

(*More shoving, and suddenly both are punching and wrestling on the floor.*)

INTERVIEWER: Break it up, fellas! Hey! Break it up!

(LIZ *comes on, now in slacks and parka, sees the fight.*)

LIZ: Oh, good Lord! (*She grabs the silver container for the champagne and pours it over the wrestlers, drenching them in snow.*) The interventionist hereby intervenes!

(*They pull apart, sputtering.*)

INTERVIEWER (*helping the* CAMERAMAN *up*): Come on, Eddie. We can still catch the end of the basketball game.

CAMERAMAN (*as they go*): If you ruined my utility belt, I'll sue your ass off!

LIZ: Bug off! Or I'll have you arrested under Title Five!

(*The TV crew goes.* LIZ *helps* COOPER *up.*)

COOPER: What's Title Five?

LIZ: I have no idea. . . . What happened?

COOPER (*putting on his jacket*): I was defending Western civilization.

LIZ: Tell me about it in the car. Where's your overcoat?

COOPER: In the checkroom.

LIZ: Wait here. I'll get it.

(*She goes out.* COOPER *looks at the empty Cotillion Room, which is now almost in darkness. The music comes up eerily.*)

COOPER (*to audience*): Kitty died in June, holding on longer than anyone expected. Good old Kitty, late at the last. Baldwin brought her back here for burial, and we had a small service down at the club. As for Jack, he made a very gentlemanly speech withdrawing from the election, and left Indiana permanently. We now hear he's running a chain of liquor stores in Phoenix, Arizona, and from all reports, doing reasonably well.

(LIZ *comes back on, hands* COOPER *his overcoat.*)

LIZ: Put this on before you catch cold.

COOPER: Thanks.

LIZ: Now give me the parking ticket. I'll bring the car around.

(*He does; she goes off.* COOPER *puts on his overcoat.*)

COOPER (*to audience*): No one ever again tried to revive the Snow Ball. It was over, done with, kaput. But as time went on, it was quite the thing to say you'd been there, at the last one, when Jack Daley danced with Kitty Price for the last time.

(*The* OLDER JACK *and* KITTY *dance upstage.*)

Okay, okay, maybe it was just a fat guy pushing an old broad around the room, but the older we got, the more we remembered a stalwart young man and a classy young woman, he proudly deliberate, she deliciously late, dancing together, on into the night. . . .

(YOUNGER JACK *and* KITTY *take over.* LIZ *comes back on.*)

LIZ: Okay. All set with the car.

COOPER: Do we have to go to the Community Center?

LIZ: Nope. Let's go home. The snow's almost stopped, by the way.

COOPER: Hand me the keys. I'll drive.

LIZ: I'd just as soon drive, Cooper.

COOPER: Come on. It'll still be slippery out there.

LIZ: Which is exactly why I should drive. . . .

(*They go off arguing as the lights fade on the young* JACK *and* KITTY *dancing beautifully downstage in a spot, as they did at the beginning.*)

(*Curtain.*)

THE OLD BOY

To John Rubinstein and Paul Benedict,
who helped me immeasurably in trying to get it right.

The Old Boy was first produced at Playwrights Horizons (André Bishop, artistic director) in New York City on May 6, 1991. It was directed by John Rubinstein; set design was by Nancy Winters; the costume design was by Jane Greenwood; the lighting design was by Nancy Schertler; the sound design was by Bruce Ellman; and the production stage manager was Michael Pule. The cast was as follows:

DEXTER *Richard Woods*
BUD *Clark Gregg*
SAM *Stephen Collins*
HARRIET *Nan Martin*
PERRY *Matt McGrath*
ALISON *Lizbeth MacKay*

The Old Boy was revised and opened at the Old Globe Theatre in San Diego, California, on January 18, 1992. It was directed by Paul Benedict; the set and lighting designs were by Kent Dorsey; the costume design was by Christine Dougherty; the sound design was by Jeff Ladman; and the production stage manager was Peter Van Dyke. The cast was as follows:

DEXTER *Franklin Cover*
BUD *Rob Neukirch*
SAM *John Getz*
HARRIET *Rosemary Murphy*
PERRY *Christopher Collet*
ALISON *Harriet Hall*

CHARACTERS

SAM, middle-aged; Under Secretary of State for Political Affairs
BUD, younger; Sam's aide
DEXTER, older; vice-rector of a distinguished private boarding
school
HARRIET, older; Perry's mother
ALISON, middle-aged; Harriet's daughter-in-law
PERRY, young; Harriet's son

SETTING

The play takes place primarily at a distinguished Episcopal boarding school in a small New England town during graduation
weekend in early June, now and in the past.

An open set, designed to accommodate a number of different
playing areas, indoors and out. Centrally located is the sitting
area of the best room in one of those old New England inns
that service the private schools near which they are located: a
few pieces of good, simple Early American furniture, particularly
a bench, which will serve as a couch, a student's bed, and ultimately the front seat of a car. Pictures of the school, or of student
teams, may be in evidence. There is also an unobtrusive bar with
liquor bottles, and a telephone somewhere else. Scene shifts are
indicated by changes in lighting and music.

ACT ONE

In darkness: the sound of a boys' choir singing:
"Brightest and best of the sons of the morning,
Dawn on our darkness, and lend us thine aid . . ."

The hymn fades into the sound of church bells chiming the hour—
4:00 P.M.—as DEXTER *enters the sitting area, followed by* BUD.
DEXTER *is in his sixties, dressed in a seersucker suit, wearing a clerical*
collar. BUD *is in his thirties, wears a summer suit, and carries an attaché*
case.

DEXTER (*proudly*): . . . And lo and behold! Our Celebrity Suite!

BUD (*looking around*): Uh-huh.

DEXTER: We keep it specially reserved for guests of the school.
  There is a bar . . . two televisions . . . *three* telephones—
  including one in the bathroom, which always struck me as
  slightly excessive. . . . Do you think this will content your
  lord and master?

BUD: It's okay.

DEXTER (*peering within*): Aha! I spy! His bags are already in the
  bedroom. I had them brought up during the press conference.

BUD: How come the press conference?

DEXTER: There seemed to be some demand.

BUD: I thought we agreed no publicity.

DEXTER: Oh, well. Our school paper . . . the local weeklies . . .

BUD: I thought we agreed.

DEXTER: Surely he can't steal in and out like a thief in the night.

BUD: I wrote you a letter. I spelled it out. This was to be a totally private visit. Then the minute we arrive, you set up mikes on the front lawn!

DEXTER: But he was proud and pleased. (*Going to a window:*) Look at him, still surrounded by students. He's enjoying himself tremendously.

BUD: What about tomorrow?

DEXTER: Tomorrow?

BUD: When he makes the commencement address. Do you plan any PR?

DEXTER: I thought possibly our local station . . .

BUD: Radio?

DEXTER: Well, actually it's a television station. . . .

BUD: You're putting him on TV?

DEXTER: Oh, just for local consumption. . . .

BUD: The answer is no.

DEXTER: No?

BUD: No TV, under any circumstances.

DEXTER: May I take the liberty of asking why?

BUD: Because he's got a good chance to be nominated governor. We don't want to broadcast the fact that he's a closet preppy, sneaking on the old school tie.

DEXTER: Oh, now really . . .

BUD: Private schools are political poison, Reverend. Take it from one who graduated from South Boston High.

DEXTER: Nonsense. Politicians are always trotting out Yale and Harvard.

BUD: Colleges are fine. You can earn your way there. But prep schools—forget it. They speak pull, they speak privilege. They go against the democratic grain.

DEXTER: Oh, yes? Well I dare say that this school, because of its large endowment and generous scholarship program, is as democratic as any high school in the country. More so, in fact, because we draw students from all over the country— indeed, all over the world! It might be time for someone to stand up and publicly point that out.

BUD: Fine. But not him. And not tomorrow. And not on TV. Are we clear on that?

(SAM *enters. He is good-looking, well-groomed, middle-aged.*)

SAM: What's the trouble?

DEXTER: I am being asked to hide your light under a bushel.

SAM: Bud is being political again?

BUD: Bud is being practical again.

SAM: Relax, Buddy. Loosen up. (*Looking around:*) And hey! What a pleasant room.

DEXTER: Henry Kissinger spent a weekend here. And Helen Hayes.

SAM: Good Lord. Together?

DEXTER: Heavens no!

BUD: That's a preppy joke.

DEXTER: Oh. Ha ha. I see . . .

SAM: Actually, I think my father stayed in this room, the week-end I graduated.

DEXTER: He may well have. Wasn't he a trustee?

SAM: He sure was. And I remember, after the ceremony, he brought me back here, sat me down in this chair, and offered me a dry martini. He said if I planned to drink, it was best I do it in front of him.

DEXTER: Ah, yes. That was the standard approach to alcohol.

SAM: I'm glad it wasn't applied to fornication.

DEXTER: What?

BUD: Another joke.

DEXTER: Oh. Ha ha. Yes. I see.

SAM: Actually, the old man was a little late, as far as liquor was concerned. Little did he know that for three years, I'd already been sneaking out with the gang after the Saturday night movie, trying to get smashed on Wildroot Cream Oil hair tonic.

DEXTER: You, Sam? Winner of the Leadership Prize?

SAM: Oh, sometimes I led in the wrong direction.

DEXTER: I shouldn't know that. Now I'll have to suspend you immediately.

SAM: Good. That gets me out of my speech tomorrow.

DEXTER: You don't want to speak? To your old alma mater?

BUD: He jumped at the chance.

SAM: That's true. . . . But now I'm here, I feel as if I'm suddenly back on the debating team, knees shaking, stomach in knots,

about to represent the school in a crucial contest against Andover. God, does anyone ever let go of this place?

DEXTER: Some of us feel it's important to hold on to.

SAM: Right. Of course. I'm sorry.

BUD: I need to phone.

(DEXTER *indicates onstage phone.*)

I'll go in there.

(*He goes off to the bedroom.*)

SAM (*looking toward the bedroom*): What a big bed! A man could
get lost in it.

DEXTER: How sad your lovely wife couldn't be here to share it
with you. Wasn't her father in the class of thirty-two?

SAM: That was my first wife.

DEXTER: Ah. Then I should have liked to meet her replacement.

SAM: She has her own agenda. You know wives these days.

DEXTER: Not well, I'm afraid.

SAM: You never married?

DEXTER: You might say I married the school. We've been together thirty-four years.

SAM: You've done better than I have. . . . (*Looking toward the
bedroom:*) Now Bud there has a nice, stay-at-home wife,
whom he's probably telephoning right now. And three sweet
kids who call me "sir" when he brings them to the office.

DEXTER: Speaking of that, what do *we* call you, when we introduce you tomorrow? Mr. Ambassador? Mr. Congressman? What?

SAM: Oh, I'll just settle for Your Majesty.

DEXTER: How about Mr. Governor?

SAM: That might be jumping the gun.

DEXTER: Oh, now. Your young friend has high hopes.

SAM: We'll see. . . . I suppose, when you have to be official, you could say Mr. Secretary. *Under* Secretary, way under, low man on the totem pole, but Secretary nonetheless. Otherwise I hope you'll just call me Sam. As you used to. When I was a boy here.

DEXTER: All right, Sam. And you should call me Dexter.

SAM: Not "Sir"? Not "Friar Tuck," which we called you behind your back?

DEXTER: Nowadays there's more alliteration involved.

SAM: I'll settle for Dexter.

DEXTER: Fine. And I'll ask the boys and girls to call you Mister.

SAM: Girls! I keep forgetting you have girls here now!

DEXTER: We have lots of things here now. We have a complete program in Asian studies. We have an active Hillel society. And we have compulsory sex education for all entering students.

SAM: Compulsory sex? Sounds better than compulsory Latin.

DEXTER: No, I meant . . .

SAM: I know what you meant, Dexter, and I'm sorry. I apologize for all my asinine remarks. Ever since I came back, I've been systematically regressing into some adolescent wise guy. You should sting me with six demerits and confine me to study hall.

DEXTER: Now, now. Just as long as you give a good speech tomorrow.

SAM: Uh-oh. What if the trumpet giveth an uncertain sound?

DEXTER: Aha! You remember your sacred studies. "If the trumpet giveth an uncertain sound, who shall prepare himself for battle?" . . . Paul. First Corinthians.

SAM: Which I just read the other night.

DEXTER: Good heavens! Since when do politicians read the Epistles of St. Paul?

SAM: When they're staying in some hotel. And can't sleep. And are tired of reading everything else. "Sounding brass and tinkling cymbal." That's me these days.

DEXTER: Oh, now.

SAM: I'm serious. I guess that's really why I came back, Dexter. I have this uncontrollable need to return to the well.

DEXTER: I'm sure we can refresh you. Remember the words of our founding rector: "No boy leaves this school unimproved."

(BUD *comes out of the bedroom.*)

BUD: I talked to the office. They say the Indonesian thing is heating up again. The White House wants you to call Jakarta and straighten things out.

SAM: Why do the Indonesians always wait till the weekend? (*He starts for the telephone.*) If you'll excuse me, Dexter . . .

DEXTER: May I just raise one other small point, before you take up scepter and crown?

SAM (*stopping*): Shoot.

DEXTER: Do you remember a boy in your class named Perry Pell?

SAM: Of course! I was his Old Boy.

BUD: His what?

DEXTER: Old Boy. It's a system we have. A student who's been here—an Old Boy—or Old Girl, these days—is assigned to a New Boy, or New Girl, and guides him, or her, through the dark wood of the first year. Sam was an Old Boy to Perry Pell. . . . (*Turning to* SAM:) Who is dead, I'm afraid.

SAM: Dead?

DEXTER: He died last winter. Some accident, apparently.

SAM: I didn't know that.

DEXTER: Neither did the alumni office. His mother just told us.

SAM: I remember his mother.

DEXTER: And she remembers you. In fact, that's why she's here.

SAM: Here?

DEXTER: She heard you were delivering the commencement address, and up she came. I think she wants you to say a few words in memory of Perry.

SAM: Glad to.

DEXTER: I told her you had a very tight schedule, but perhaps she could stop by for a drink around five-thirty, before we submit to the evening's festivities. I'll officiate, of course.

SAM: Fine with me.

DEXTER: Frankly, if I may speak briefly of treasures laid up on earth, she has proposed a major gift to the school in Perry's name.

SAM: Big bucks?

DEXTER: An indoor tennis facility. Two courts, a viewer's gallery, locker facilities—for both sexes, of course. She hopes you'll announce it tomorrow as well.

SAM: Of course. . . . Did Perry's wife come along, by any chance?

DEXTER: Actually, yes. You knew her?

SAM: She was my date for the senior dance. That's how he met her.

DEXTER: What a small world!

SAM: It was then . . .

DEXTER: Well, now, I'll leave you to render unto Caesar the things that are Caesar's.

(*He goes.*)

SAM (*broodingly*): Perry Pell . . .

BUD: Sam.

SAM: Mmmm? Oh. All right. The Indonesian thing . . . (*He starts again for the phone.*)

BUD: This stinks, Sam.

SAM: Now, now.

BUD: This sucks, man. I'm serious. I don't like this gig.

SAM: Something wrong with your room, Bud?

BUD: Sure. Per usual, they put me over the parking lot.

SAM: I'll tell them to change it.

BUD: They're using you, Sam.

SAM: Oh, come on . . .

BUD: They're taking advantage! I make the deal, in and out, a quiet weekend in New England. And now suddenly you're giving cocktail parties, and announcing indoor tennis courts, and doing preppy press conferences on the front lawn!

SAM: That's the first press conference I ever enjoyed.

BUD: And you got so chuckly and nostalgic I almost puked.

SAM: Easy, Bud.

BUD: Sam, we're running for the roses here! You have a clear track, all the way to November! There's only one little hitch in the whole picture, Sam.

SAM: And what is that, Bud, as if I didn't know.

BUD: The preppy thing.

SAM (*making it grimly portentous*): The Preppy Thing.

BUD: No one likes WASPs anymore, Sam.

SAM: The Irish adore us.

BUD: Not always, man. It's a love-hate thing.

SAM: You're Irish, Bud, and you love me.

BUD: I do love you—I mean, not *love* you, like you . . . No, all right, love you. Don't tell Katie, but I do. I think you're the most decent guy I ever met. I'm betting on you, Sam. Which is why I quit my law firm, and took a salary cut of twenty grand, and am holed up here all weekend, overlooking a parking lot, rather than home with Katie and the kids. I mean, it bugs me, Sam! You were all signed up! Keynote speech at the National Conference of Mayors. Network coverage, hot issues, strong party support. Then Dexter calls, and you opt for this. People are pissed, Sam.

SAM: I know that.

BUD: Maybe you *don't* know how much I had to cover your ass, Sam. I piled story on top of story.

SAM: I appreciate it, Bud. Really.

BUD: Yeah, well, then what's the *real* story? Any thoughts? Now you're here?

SAM: I don't know. Maybe I'm like an Atlantic salmon. I got a whiff of those old headwaters and just had to head upstream.

BUD: Don't salmon die when they do that?

SAM (*laughing*): *Pacific* salmon do, Bud. The Atlantic salmon tends to survive. . . . Oh, hell, all I know is that there's something here. Something I missed, or lost, or need. Something I had to look for.

BUD: Then look for it *quietly*, okay?

SAM: Which means?

BUD: Which means don't stand up tomorrow, after you've reneged on a great speech on the problems of urban America, and in your best George Plimpton accent focus on a fancy tennis facility dedicated to some geek named Perry Pell. Please, Sam. That, don't do.

SAM: I—intend to pay my respects to a good friend.

BUD: Sometimes I think you don't want to win, Sam.

SAM: Sometimes I don't.

BUD: You'd better call the Indonesians.

SAM (*stretching out on the couch*): Suppose you take over the Pacific Rim this weekend.

BUD: What'll I say?

SAM: Say we deeply deplore whatever it is they're doing.

BUD: That won't wash.

SAM: Then tell them to do it our way.

BUD: They don't want to.

SAM: Then say the check is in the mail.

BUD (*taking his attaché case*): That'll fly. I'll be in my room. (*He starts out, stops, turns.*) Don't get caught in this shit, Sam. Really. You've got too much to lose.

SAM: The past has a way of sneaking up on you, Bud.

BUD: So does the future. . . .

(*He goes off, as music comes up: a boys' choir singing: "Oh Paradise, oh Paradise . . ." SAM gets up, takes off his jacket, looks out. Greenery and bird sounds.*)

SAM (*now younger; calling out*): Come on, you guys! Many hands make light work! . . . Keep going! . . . Rake 'em into three main piles!

(HARRIET PELL *appears in autumn light. She is a classy woman, with neat hair, wearing conventional, expensive clothes in the style of the early sixties. She calls to* SAM.)

HARRIET: You there! Young man! May I speak to you, please?

SAM: Excuse me?

HARRIET: I'm looking for the young man in charge of the work program.

SAM: That's me.

HARRIET: Then you're our Old Boy! (*Calling off to* PERRY.) I've found Sam, Perry! I've found our Old Boy! (*To* SAM:) I'm already impressed. Making all those boys do all that work.

SAM: We all have to pitch in. It creates a sense of community.

HARRIET: Well, I want to create a sense of Perry Pell. (*She calls off again.*) Perry! We're waiting!

(PERRY *comes on reluctantly. He is young, dressed in jacket and tie.*)

Perry, this is Sam. Shake hands, Perry. Good, firm grip. Look him right in the eye.

(*The boys shake hands.* PERRY *moves away.*)

That's Perry, Sam. And I'm his mother. (*She holds out her hand.*)

SAM (*shaking hands with her*): I figured.

HARRIET: I was very particular about selecting Perry's Old Boy. I asked for someone of the same age, in the same class, but who's been here a year. I want someone who plays sports *well*, and has recognizable leadership qualities. You obviously fill the bill.

SAM: Thanks.

HARRIET: I understand your father went here.

SAM: He's a trustee, actually. And my grandfather went here. And two uncles.

HARRIET: Mercy! You *are* an Old Boy! See, Perry? Sam knows the ropes, up and down the line. He'll help you fit in.

SAM: I'll sure try.

HARRIET: Now, Sam, you should know that Perry is an only child.

PERRY (*quietly*): Mother . . .

HARRIET: No, darling. Sam should know that. He should also know that your father is totally out of the picture. (*To* SAM:) I've had to take over from scratch in that department.

PERRY: Come on, Mother. . . .

HARRIET: Sam should know these things, dear. So he can whip you into shape.

PERRY: You forgot to tell him I'm toilet trained.

(*He exits again.*)

HARRIET (*laughing nervously*): He has an unusual sense of humor. (*Looks off.*) But he retreats. He withdraws. He backs away. He goes to Washington with his school to visit the major monuments, ends up alone at the movies. He gets invited to his first formal dance last Christmas, winds up in a corner, reading a book. He reaches the semifinals of our local tennis tournament, and what? Defaults, so he can go to New York and visit his father.

SAM: Would he have won the tennis tournament?

HARRIET: No, Sam. No. I do not think he would have won. I think he would have lost. Because he refuses to go to the net.

SAM: No net game, huh?

HARRIET: No net game, Sam. Neither in tennis nor in life. I'll bet you have a net game.

(*They might sit together on the bench.*)

SAM: Don't have much else.

HARRIET: Well, Sam, you and I know, in our deep heart's core, that sooner or later people have to run to the net, and put the ball away. Otherwise, they lose. I hope your parents tell you the same thing.

SAM: My mother's given up tennis. She's not too well, actually.

HARRIET: Oh, dear. Nothing serious, I hope.

SAM: I hope. . . .

HARRIET (*looking off*): Look at Perry, standing by that lake. Watch. Soon he'll start skipping stones.

(*They watch.*)

See? That sort of thing can go on for hours! I'm all for marching to a different drummer, but this one won't march at all!

(*Chapel chimes are heard. She gets up.*)

Well. I suppose it's time to go. (*Calls off.*) I'm leaving, darling!
Time for the changing of the guard. (*To* SAM:) Look how he
walks. Just like his father. Who now slouches around Green-
wich Village, calling himself an artist.

(PERRY *comes on again.*)

Shoulders back, darling. And goodbye. (*Kisses him.*) Be strong,
write lots of letters, and pay attention to your Old Boy.
(*Shakes hands with* SAM.) Goodbye, Sam. I'm counting on you.

(*She kisses* PERRY *again and goes.*)
      (*Pause. The boys look at each other.*)

SAM: Where's your stuff?

(*No answer.*)

Where's your stuff, Perry?

PERRY (*very quietly*): Over at the dorm.

SAM: What?

PERRY (*louder*): Over at the dorm.

SAM: Met your roommate?

PERRY: Yeah.

SAM: Like him?

PERRY: He's okay.

SAM: What about your bed?

PERRY: What about it?

SAM: Made your bed yet?

PERRY: No.

SAM: Come on. We'll go down to the dorm and make your bed.

PERRY: I don't want to make my bed.

SAM: You've got to make your bed, Perry. They have inspections. You get demerits.

PERRY (*almost inaudibly*): I don't think I'm right for this place.

SAM: Huh?

PERRY (*shouting*): I DON'T THINK I'M RIGHT FOR THIS PLACE!

SAM: Sssh! Hey. Go easy.

PERRY: I think I've made a serious mistake.

SAM: New boys always say that.

PERRY: No, it's not right for me. I can tell. Guys are playing hockey with Coke cans in the halls. I got stuck with the upper bunk. My roommate treats records like shit. . . .

SAM: The first day always feels that way.

PERRY: No, I can tell when I'm not right for things. I wasn't right for boxing lessons. I wasn't right for Wilderness Camp.

SAM: I hear you're a great tennis player, though.

PERRY: I'm okay. . . . Do guys ever run away from this place?

SAM: Not really.

PERRY: I might do it.

SAM: Run *away*?

PERRY: I might.

SAM: Where to?

PERRY: New York.

SAM: New *York*?

PERRY: Where my dad lives.

SAM: You'd live with your dad?

PERRY: I'll get my own place.

SAM: In New *York*? It's hugely expensive.

PERRY: I've got money. And I'll get a job.

SAM: Hey, wow! You mean you'd just . . . (*Pause.*) Well, you can't.

PERRY: Why not?

SAM: You need an education, Perry.

PERRY: My grandfather quit school after seventh grade, and made sixty million dollars. Where do you get a taxi around here? (*He starts off.*)

SAM: If you try to shove off, Perry, I'd have to turn you right in.

PERRY: Why?

SAM: Because . . . (*Pause.*) Because I'm your Old Boy. I'm responsible for you.

PERRY: Just say you didn't know.

SAM: Nope. Can't. I promised your mother.

PERRY: Then I'll wait for another time.

SAM: Let's sit down for a minute. (*He indicates the bench.*)

PERRY: I don't want to sit down.

SAM: Just sit. It doesn't hurt to sit—unless you have hemor-
rhoids.

(PERRY *doesn't sit.*)

At least look out at the Lower School pond.

(*More bird sounds.*)

PERRY: I'm looking.

SAM: I noticed earlier you were skipping stones on that pond.

PERRY: And?

SAM: Didn't it kind of calm you down? Doing that?

PERRY: Maybe.

SAM: Know why?

PERRY: Why?

SAM: You were connecting with nature.

PERRY: Get serious.

SAM: I *am* serious, Perry. Consider what you can do with that
pond. You can skinny-dip in it, up by the dam. You can play
hockey on it in the winter. You can build a raft on it in the
spring. You can connect with it all during the school year.
And whenever you do, you're connecting with nature, Perry.
And when you connect with nature, it makes you a better
guy.

PERRY: Save it for Sunday, okay?

SAM: No, it's true. I'm going to tell you something personal now. When I was a kid, I dreaded going here. I mean, my father entered me at birth, for God's sake. I had no choice, even for another boarding school. My mom wanted me to stay at country day, but he vetoed the proposition. This was it. And when it came time to come, he just put me on the bus. My mom wasn't allowed to drive me up, because *his* mom didn't. "Throw him in the water and he'll swim," my dad said. And the day I left, my mom and I were both crying, but he wouldn't even let us do *that*. I mean, your mom at least came *with* you.

PERRY: Don't remind me.

SAM: Anywhere, here I was, stuck here, and at first I felt really low. So I took it out on people. I took it out on fat guys, for example. I'd tease them and grab their tits and all that. I mean, I was a real shit. But then I took a good long walk around the Lower School pond, and connected with nature, and now I honestly feel I'm a better guy.

PERRY: I don't mind fat guys.

SAM: Neither do I. Now. I *like* them, in fact. That's my point. And that's just an example of what happens here. What also happens is you get the finest education in the United States. You read Cicero in Latin in your Fourth Form year. You study European history, right on up to World War One. You read Shakespeare and Chaucer with the dirty parts left in.

PERRY: What dirty parts?

SAM: "The hand of time is on the prick of noon." How about that?

PERRY (*sarcastically*): Oh, I'm shocked! I'm disgusted!

SAM: Okay, so it doesn't hit you. So we'll shift to sports. Consider the athletic program.

PERRY: I read the catalogue, Sam.

SAM: All I'm saying, this is one great school. Guys all over the country are knocking themselves out to come here. The sons of two United States senators go here. The head of General Motors has his grandson right here. Katharine Hepburn's nephew goes here, and a kid whose mother was married to Ty Cobb. There are Jewish guys here now, and they raise the level of discourse, and Negroes on scholarship, who are a credit to their race. There are foreigners here, too—Japanese, and South Americans, and a kid from Hungary who took on Communist *tanks*! Oh, I'm telling you, Perry, if the Russians dropped a bomb on this place, it would cripple the entire free world!

PERRY: Aren't you slightly overdoing it?

SAM: Okay, but everyone here is a privileged person. And we have a responsibility to stay. We have a responsibility to take the courses, and go to chapel, and improve our bodies and our minds. That way, we become leading citizens. So if you ran away, you'd be turning your back on society and yourself.

PERRY: All you're saying is go make your bed. Right?

(*Pause.*)

SAM: Right. (*He laughs.*) I'm full of shit sometimes, aren't I?

PERRY: Yeah, well, who isn't?

SAM: No, but I sometimes get carried away. I'm glad you brought it to my attention, Perry. You'll be good for me. Just as I'll be good for you. Now. What about that bed?

PERRY: I guess I'll make it.

SAM: And I'll help you, Perry. And then we'll stir up a game of Frisbee.

PERRY: I stink at Frisbee.

SAM: We'll deal with that, Perry. We'll work on that. Meanwhile, do you know how to make hospital corners?

PERRY: No, frankly.

SAM: I'll show you how to make hospital corners.

(*They run out. Another hymn: "Rise up, Oh Men of God." DEXTER enters, carrying a tray of glasses, an ice bucket, and some potato chips.*)

DEXTER: Room service, room service, courtesy of the school!

SAM'S VOICE (*from within*): Be right out!

DEXTER (*crossing to the bar*): No tipping, please! (*He sets the tray down, calls off the other way.*) Ladies! I believe the governor is ready to convene the legislature.

(HARRIET *and* ALISON *come in.* HARRIET *now looks older and wears contemporary clothes.* ALISON *is attractive and also well dressed.*)

HARRIET (*looking around*): What a lovely room! Somewhat larger than those cubicles we've been assigned to!

(SAM *enters, putting on his jacket and tie.*)

SAM: Welcome, welcome.

HARRIET (*going to him*): Oh, Sam! Dear boy! How good to see you again! (*She embraces him warmly.*)

SAM: I'm so sorry about Perry, Mrs. Pell.

HARRIET: He adored you, Sam. He kept clippings from your whole career.

ALISON: Hello, Sam.

SAM: Alison.

(*They kiss on the cheek.*)

DEXTER (*officiating with the drinks*): Now, who'll have what? Mrs. Pell?

HARRIET: Oh, let's see. It's June, isn't it? I think I might be talked into a gin and tonic.

DEXTER: Gin and tonic it is.

HARRIET (*leading* SAM *to the bench*): Now, sit here, Sam. Next to me.

DEXTER (*to* ALISON): Mrs. Pell, Jr.?

ALISON: Just club soda, please. (*She sits off to one side.*)

DEXTER: A little wine, for thy stomach's sake?

ALISON: No thank you. No.

DEXTER: Sam?

SAM: Light scotch, please, Dexter.

HARRIET: "Light scotch, please." I remember that very well. When you stopped by Grosse Pointe on your way west with Perry. Always light scotch.

SAM: Sometimes it wasn't so light.

HARRIET: Oh, Sam, you've never gone overboard in your life.

ALISON: Oh, yes he has.

(SAM, HARRIET, *and* DEXTER *look at her.*) Long ago and far away.

HARRIET: Oh, well, we all lose our grip occasionally. I did when I got married. But I came to my senses fast, let me tell you.

DEXTER: Sam, where's your ubiquitous amanuensis?

SAM: Who? Oh, you mean Bud.

DEXTER: Won't he join the dance?

SAM: Bud's in his room, proving that most of the important work in government is done by junior members of the staff.

ALISON: Isn't your wife here?

SAM: Couldn't make it.

HARRIET: Oh, dear. And I hear she's perfectly lovely. She was a Thayer, wasn't she? From Philadelphia.

SAM: That was my first wife.

HARRIET: You traded her in?

SAM: Three years ago.

ALISON: The new one's name is Carol, and she has two children by her first marriage, just as you have two by yours, and you live in an old brick row house in Georgetown, where she runs a real estate office, and you serve the country at home and abroad.

SAM: Good for you.

ALISON: Oh, I keep up.

SAM: You know more about me than I know about you.

ALISON: What's to know?

HARRIET: I'll tell you what's to know: Alison and Perry lived
a lovely life together. They produced a sweet boy—my dear
grandson . . . (*To* DEXTER:) Who I hope will be admitted to
this school the year after next.

ALISON: He's certainly been admitted to enough others.

HARRIET (*to* DEXTER): He has minor behavior problems.

ALISON: Which are threatening to become major.

HARRIET: He's in military school at the moment.

ALISON: Which he hates.

HARRIET: Which is ironing out a few wrinkles.

ALISON: If not burning a few holes.

DEXTER: I'm sure we can find a place for him, Mrs. Pell.

ALISON: If he wants to come.

HARRIET: How do they know what they want at that age? They
must be pointed, they must be pushed.

ALISON: He might do better if he chose.

DEXTER (*passing a plate*): Potato chips, anyone? They're all I
could drum up.

SAM: You look like you're serving Holy Communion, Dexter.

DEXTER: What? Oh, dear. Ha ha. That's two demerits, for
blasphemy.

HARRIET: Sam, I want to tell you about Perry. (*Pause.*) It was
a ghastly mistake. He misread his prescription, and took all
the wrong pills.

ALISON: Oh . . .

HARRIET: Alison, of course, has a different opinion.

ALISON: The doctor has a different opinion.

HARRIET: Doctors don't know! I know Perry. I know that he'd never intentionally leave us without even saying goodbye. No. I'm sorry. No.

SAM: I'm sorry, too, Mrs. Pell.

HARRIET: I wish you'd been there, Sam. To keep him up to the mark.

SAM: We kind of lost touch after school.

HARRIET: He loved you, Sam. He loved this school. It was a turning point in his life.

DEXTER: That's why your gift will be so appropriate, Mrs. Pell.

HARRIET: He loved tennis, Sam.

ALISON: Well, he didn't *love* it.

HARRIET: He won the tennis trophy!

ALISON: He liked other things more.

HARRIET: He won the tennis trophy here at school! He played on the varsity at college!

ALISON: But he gave it up.

HARRIET: He loved the game, Alison. We watched Wimbledon together. Now stop contradicting.

ALISON: I wish . . . oh, well.

SAM: What, Alison?

ALISON: I wish, instead of this tennis thing, it could be something to do with music.

HARRIET: As a memorial? For *Perry*?

ALISON: He loved music.

HARRIET: Couldn't play a note.

ALISON: He loved listening to it.

HARRIET: Music lessons for six years. Down the drain.

ALISON: But he listened to music all the time. What if there
were some sort of place, with comfortable chairs, and good
books all around, and a music collection, where people could
put on earphones and listen to music, or read, or even sleep,
if they wanted to?

HARRIET: That sounds very much like retreating to me.

ALISON: But Perry'd love a place like that.

HARRIET: That sounds like unconditional surrender.

ALISON: But—

HARRIET: I say tennis, Alison. And I happen to be paying the
bill.

ALISON (*to* SAM): You can see how my mother-in-law and I get
along.

HARRIET: Ah, but we always understand each other in the end,
don't we, dear?

ALISON: I'm afraid we do.

HARRIET (*looking around*): I suppose you all think I'm a superficial woman simply interested in a snobby game.

DEXTER: Oh, no. Heavens, no. Mercy, not at all.

HARRIET: Well, let me tell you something about tennis. When I was a girl, I was taught the game, and one of the things I learned was that every set, every game, every point is a new chance. As opposed to golf. There you are doomed from the start. Do badly on the first hole, you carry your mistakes on your back forever.

DEXTER: I see! What you're saying is that there is infinite salvation in tennis! Like Catholicism. Whereas golf is Protestant and predestined.

HARRIET: I don't know about that. I do know that when I was young, I made a mistake. I married the wrong man. But because I played *tennis*, I didn't feel I had to live with him for the rest of my life. I said "All right, I've lost the first set. Time to change courts and start again." That's what I learned from tennis. And that's what Perry learned. And that's what I want the boys and girls at this school to learn, by playing tennis all year round. (*With a glance at* ALISON:) Rather than slinking off into some corner to listen to what? *La Forza del Destino?* Am I right or am I right, Sam?

SAM: Perhaps we shouldn't decide tonight.

ALISON: And the former ambassador to Iceland once again exercises diplomatic immunity.

DEXTER: We *do* have to decide whether or not to have our second drink here, or at Hargate, where the rector and his lady are waiting to greet us.

SAM: Let's go.

DEXTER: And then we'll proceed to the main dining room, where we will sup at the head table. Then, following our repast, and after the ladies have had a chance to powder their noses, we will attend the spring production of *All's Well That Ends Well.*

HARRIET (*taking* SAM's *arm as they go*): Poor Sam. You're stuck with us all evening.

SAM: All the more chance to hear about Perry.

DEXTER (*to* ALISON): After you, Mrs. Pell.

ALISON (*who has been staring off*): What? Who? Oh, right, I keep forgetting that's me. Thank you.

(*She goes out, followed by* DEXTER, *as the music comes up: the Overture to* La Forza del Destino. PERRY *enters, in sweater and slacks, reciting, occasionally referring to a paperback playbook. He is very good.*)

PERRY:
      "My father had a daughter lov'd a man
      As it might be perhaps, were I woman,
      I should your lordship. . . .
            She never told her love,
      But let concealment like a worm i' th' bud
      Feed on her damask cheek. . . .
      We men may say more, swear more; but indeed
      Our shows are more than will; for still we prove
      Much in our vows, but little in our love."

(SAM *enters, now wearing a sweater, hockey skates slung over his shoulder.*)

SAM (*gesturing toward the "record player"*): Turn down the Farts of Destiny, will ya?

PERRY (*going to turn it off*): *The Force of Destiny*, Sam. *La Forza del Destino*. Jesus. You and that joke. We've heard it too many times.

SAM: We've heard the Farts of Destiny too many times. Bruiser MacLane says you're driving him batty with that record.

PERRY: He plays "Moon River" night and day.

SAM: That's different. Yours is an opera.

PERRY: What's wrong with opera?

SAM: Bruiser says it's fifty percent fag.

PERRY: Oh, come on . . .

SAM: He *knows*, Perry. He's from San Francisco!

PERRY: Stop playing Old Boy, Sam. That was last year, okay?

(SAM *throws himself on the "bed."*)

SAM: Okay. Fine. Play what you want. Who gives a shit?

PERRY: What's eating you?

SAM: Nothing. (*Pause.*) Except I just got a call from the old man.

PERRY: And?

SAM: He can't take me skiing at Stowe spring vacation.

PERRY: Why not?

SAM: Too expensive. He *says*. But I think he's got a girl.

PERRY: Well, that happens. I mean, your mom's been gone almost a year.

SAM: I know it happens, Perry. I'm not dumb. (*Pause.*) I also know he doesn't love me.

PERRY: Oh, come on. . . .

SAM: He *likes* me. But he doesn't love me. I used to think if I did well, if I won prizes and stuff, maybe he'd love me. But now I wonder.

PERRY: At least he leaves you alone.

SAM: Look, your mother wants the best for you because she thinks you deserve it. My dad thinks I'll never really measure up. That's the difference. (*Pause.*) Anyway. Spring vacation. Maybe I'll come south and hook up with you.

PERRY: Actually, I'll be in New York spring vacation.

SAM: I thought the tennis team planned to practice in South Carolina.

PERRY: I'm not playing tennis this year.

SAM: *What?*

PERRY: I decided to be in the spring show.

SAM: Do both, for God's sake.

PERRY: Can't. I got a lead role, and the tennis team has too many games away.

SAM: But you're due to play second on the varsity this year!

PERRY: That's the way the ball bounces.

SAM: All I can say is it better be one hell of a good play.

PERRY: It's Shakespeare.

SAM: Oh, God, not again. What play?

PERRY: *Twelfth Night*, actually.

SAM: That's not such a great play, Perry. I got a C minus on that one.

PERRY: I like it. A lot.

SAM: You playing that duke?

PERRY: No, actually not.

SAM: Then who? One of those clowns who think they're so funny?

PERRY: Actually, I'm playing Viola.

SAM: Viola? You mean the *girl*?

PERRY: She's a boy all during the play.

SAM: But she's really a girl.

PERRY: She wears pants all the way through.

SAM: But she is definitely a *girl*, Perry.

PERRY: Okay, she's a girl.

SAM: You played a girl last year.

PERRY: I played Mercutio last year.

SAM: You also played a girl.

PERRY: In the musical. Because they asked me to. I won the prize for Mercutio.

SAM: Perry, let me say something here. Now, how do I put this? You and I are good friends now, right?

PERRY: Right.

SAM: I mean, we're way beyond last year's Old Boy shit. I mean, when my mother died, and I wanted to bug out, *you* were the Old Boy, actually. You got me to stay.

PERRY: Misery loves company.

SAM: Yeah, well, we're even. This is just friends talking. Friend to friend. And I'm not saying this just for an excuse to go south spring vacation, either. What I'm saying is I really don't think you should take that part in that play, Perry.

PERRY: Here beginneth today's bullshit.

SAM: No, but remember last year? That Fairy Perry stuff?

PERRY: That's over now.

SAM: Because of your *tennis* it's over! I'm telling you, you play another girl, and keep up this opera crap, it'll start up again! It's a bird, it's a plane, it's Fairy Perry!

PERRY: Knock it off, okay.

SAM: They even called *me* a fairy for hanging out with you. That's how I got in that fight that time. I was defending *both* of us.

PERRY: I can defend myself, Sam.

SAM: You'll have to, if you take that part.

PERRY: Fat Pig Hathaway gets those pig jokes all the time. Piggy-piggy. Soo-ey. Oink, oink. He lives through it.

SAM: What you don't know is, Perry, Fat Pig had to see a psychiatrist last summer. He had to cancel a canoe trip.

PERRY: Alas and alack.

SAM: I'm *serious*, for chrissake. The choices you make in school are extremely significant, Perry. They can have an important effect on your later life.

PERRY: Okay. Now apply the bullshit quotient . . . divide that by two point five . . .

SAM: Oh, hell. I give up.

(*Pause.*)

PERRY: In Shakespeare's time, boys played all the girls' parts.

SAM: I know that.

PERRY: Same with the Greeks. Same on up to the seventeenth century. Guys played girls all the time.

SAM: Who doesn't know that?

PERRY: Yeah, well, no one ran around calling them fairies, Sam. They were considered first-rate guys. Actors from Athens served as ambassadors to Sparta.

SAM: No wonder Athens lost the war.

PERRY: Ha ha. Big joke. Remind me to laugh sometime.

SAM: I just can't believe you like acting better than tennis.

PERRY: I like—being someone else.

SAM: It's kind of weird, when you think about it, Perry.

PERRY: Maybe I'm weird then.

SAM: Well, people who are weird work on the problem. They try *not* to be weird.

PERRY: Maybe I like being weird. Ever think of that?

SAM: Didn't you like it when you beat that guy from Exeter in the JV match last year? Three great sets, the last one ten–eight. Didn't you like that?

PERRY: I loved that!

SAM: Yeah, but it's not weird enough, huh. So you're going to give up a major slot on the varsity tennis team, which could make you captain next year. Which could get you into Columbia, which is in New York City, your favorite place. Which won't happen if your grades go down because you spend too much time rehearsing plays, playing a girl. (*Pause.* SAM *looks at his watch.*) Well, I'm late for the debating society. Maybe I'll do better over there. (*Starts out.*)

PERRY: Sam.

(SAM *stops.*)

You did okay.

SAM (*coming back in*): If you played tennis, we could end up in Florida. We could check out the Yanks in spring training! Your favorite team, man!

PERRY: Get going, Sam.

(SAM *starts out again, then stops again.*)

SAM: I just wish you'd talk to Bruiser MacLane, that's all. He'll tell you about *real* fairies. Guys who look at you in the men's room. Guys who—

PERRY: Get out of here, Sam!

SAM: Okay, but think tennis, man!

(SAM *runs off, as* PERRY *stands looking after him. He gets his Shakespeare book, ponders it, then goes slowly off, as a hymn comes up:* "Creations, Lord." *It becomes dark on stage.* BUD, *in his shirtsleeves, comes in, holding a fax sheet.*)

BUD (*toward bedroom*): Sam? (*He turns on a light, goes to the tele-phone, dials quickly.*) Hi. It's me. . . . Give me Bill again . . . Bill, I just picked up your fax down at the desk. Now listen: you checked this out, right? I don't want to go out on a limb here, man. . . . You're sure then?

(SAM *comes in from the hall.*)

Uh-huh . . . uh-huh . . . Thanks. I'll return the favor, Bill. (*He hangs up.*)

SAM: Still burning the midnight oil, Bud? I thought we were all to make a conscious effort to conserve energy.

BUD: How was *All's Well That Ends Well*?

SAM: Fine, except for the ending.

BUD: This fax just came in from Washington.

SAM: About Indonesia?

BUD: About your friend . . . how he died.

SAM (*taking it*): Thinking of transferring to the FBI, Bud?

BUD: You asked.

SAM: I didn't ask *you*.

BUD: I happened to have a call in to Treasury. The guy on night security ran a quick check.

SAM: I know how he died, Bud.

BUD: I don't think you do.

SAM (*reads, looks up*): AIDS?

BUD: Suicide. Because of AIDS. Made it look like an accident. To make it easy on his family.

SAM: You sure?

BUD: I double-checked.

(*Pause.*)

SAM: Go to bed, Bud.

BUD: Still plan to make a speech about this guy?

SAM: Of course.

BUD: You still plan to make a speech, at a posh prep school, with the primary right down the road, at a time when people who are HIV-positive can no longer get into the *country*, about a close friend who died of AIDS?

SAM: I said I would.

BUD: If our friends on the right get wind of this . . .

SAM: I'll deal with that.

BUD: Let me write it, then.

SAM: You didn't know him.

BUD: All the better.

SAM: Bud . . .

BUD: This is a minefield, Sam.

(*Knocking from offstage.*)

  Christ. Who's that? Jesse Helms?

SAM (*calling*): Come in.

(ALISON *comes in.*)

ALISON: Am I interrupting something?

BUD: Looks like I am.

SAM: Bud's going to bed.

BUD: Bud's going to work.

(*He leaves.*)

ALISON: I'm sure he thought I was here to seduce you.

SAM: Why would he think that?

ALISON: Because that's what I plan to do.

SAM: Damn! I planned to seduce *you*.

ALISON: We can take turns.

SAM: I take it you got my little note.

ALISON: Found it under my door.

SAM: I figured the bar downstairs was about to close, and since I have this sitting room . . .

ALISON: Absolutely. And I got Harriet to go straight to bed. I heard her snoring like a soldier when I tiptoed past her door.

SAM: May she dream of Swedish tennis stars, all running to the net.

ALISON: Amen.

SAM: So. Here we are.

ALISON: The Old Boy and his Old Girl. . . . Do you ever think about those days?

SAM: I'm thinking about them now.

ALISON: That summer on Martha's Vineyard . . .

SAM: Ah. The Vineyard . . .

ALISON: No cracks, please. It was home to me. My father ran the hardware store, remember?

SAM: What I remember is the sail locker of the Edgartown Yacht Club.

ALISON: Don't rush things.

SAM: You're right. If I'm going to reseduce you, I should ply you with alcohol.

ALISON: The way you did then? With scotch? Stolen from the Yacht Club bar?

SAM: What'll you have this time?

ALISON: Nothing, thanks.

SAM: Given it up?

ALISON: Trying to.

SAM: You and everyone else in the postindustrial world. Makes it tougher to seduce people. (*Makes himself a drink.*) You look terrific, by the way.

ALISON: Do I look to the manor born?

SAM: You sure do.

ALISON: Good. I've been working on it since the day we met.

SAM: Do you remember that day?

ALISON: Totally. I was waitressing at the Clamshell, earning money for college.

SAM: And I was visiting Kip Farraday, from school.

ALISON: Whoever. I never knew your names. All I knew was you moved in a flock. The annual migration, the June arrival of the summer boys, with your white teeth, and old sneakers, and no socks, and great wads of money stuffed in your Bermuda shorts.

SAM: Not much in mine.

ALISON: No. You were different. The flock blew into the Clamshell, and blew out, but you stayed. And ordered another cheeseburger. And introduced yourself.

SAM: And asked you to the movies . . .

ALISON: And to the beach the next day. But I'll have you know it took you a week to get me into that sail locker.

SAM: Do you remember I rigged up a bed for us with someone's silk spinnaker?

ALISON: I remember everything. That was my first time.

SAM: Mine, too.

ALISON: I know. (*Pause.*) It was a lot of firsts. It was the first time I began to wonder where you came from, you summer boys. Suddenly all I wanted in the world was to get off that island, and see where you went after Labor Day.

SAM: And so you did.

ALISON: Yes I did. Thanks to you. What a gentleman you were! Inviting me up here for that dance. That was another thing summer boys didn't do.

SAM: I hope you had a good time.

ALISON: Oh, I did! (*Pause.*) No, I didn't. (*Pause.*) My shoes were wrong. (*Pause. She looks at her feet.*) Well, they're right now, goddammit.

SAM (*getting close to her*): I like the shoes.

ALISON: Thank you.

SAM (*nuzzling her*): I like what's in them.

ALISON: Still the same old line, I see.

SAM: Sure you won't have a drink?

ALISON: No thanks. I'm not an alcoholic, I don't think, but liquor gets me going.

SAM: All the more reason.

ALISON: I think we should talk about Perry.

SAM: I know about Perry.

ALISON: The whole story?

SAM: Enough. Bud did some homework. Are you all right?

ALISON: Me? Oh, you mean my health? Sure. Fine. I had myself thoroughly tested. It was unlikely, anyway. We hadn't slept together for years. So you see it's perfectly safe for you to be seduced.

SAM: Poor Alison.

ALISON: No, actually, *not* poor Alison. Rich Alison, which was what I wanted. They say if you marry money, you end up earning every cent of it.

SAM: Was it grim?

ALISON: Not for a while. We had one hell of a good time at first. Perry was lavishly affectionate. And we had great fun. We bought this gorgeous house outside of town, had horses, dogs, even a baby. Money does a lot, Sam. It kept us going for quite a while. Until he announced he was gay.

SAM: Announced?

ALISON: Sat me down one day, and told me point blank. And I said, "Oh, don't be silly—just because our sex life is a little dicey lately," so then he said he'd just made love with the man who cleaned the pool. I remember hearing that goddamn *Forza del Destino* blaring away in the background.

SAM: Oh, boy.

ALISON: So I said get out. Darken our poolhouse no more. Something like that. (*Pause.*) Do you think I would have said that if it had been a woman? (*Pause.*) I know he never said it when I'd been with men. (*Pause.*) Maybe I will have a drink after all.

SAM: You're sure, now?

(*Chapel chimes are heard.*)

ALISON: I am sure. How about rye and ginger, for old times sake?

SAM: There's neither one.

ALISON: Then vodka. Straight. Thanks.

(SAM *pours it.*)

Aaanyway, off he went, into outer darkness. And then came the explosion. He must have been building up steam all along. Lover after lover after . . . But did I get divorced? Not this cookie! Oh, no. I bided my time. Why? Money. Harriet paid the hush money, or whatever you want to call it. And I was free to continue a few discreet relationships of my own. Then, when he got sick, I couldn't . . . I mean, I couldn't just . . . I mean, he was *dying*.

SAM: Were you . . . hey, do you mind these questions?

ALISON: I like them. You're the first person who's had the guts to ask.

SAM: Were you with him when he died?

ALISON: No. By then, he had found his one true love. In his precious New York. A dear man who runs a travel agency. And who took care of him. And helped with the pills. And came to the funeral. And cried. Well, we all cried.

SAM: Poor guy. Not even saying goodbye . . .

ALISON: I know. That sweet man. We loved each other, in a way. In a good way. Of course, it wasn't . . . the way he felt about his final friend. Or the way I felt about you.

SAM: Uh-oh.

ALISON: Oh, no. Don't worry. We played that scene out years ago. Remember? The old Whaler Bar, on Madison Avenue, the day after Labor Day? Me tossing down rye and gingers and spilling my guts all over the table. You sipping your goddamn scotch. And spurning me.

SAM: I didn't "spurn" you, Alison.

ALISON: You said you didn't love me.

SAM: I said I didn't love you enough.

ALISON: Enough for what, for God's sake?

SAM: Enough to stay faithful, at different colleges, all the next year. Enough to get married after we graduated. Which is what you wanted.

ALISON: Your father didn't like me.

SAM: He didn't know you.

ALISON: He didn't want to know me.

SAM: He didn't think I was ready to get involved.

ALISON: But Perry was.

SAM: Seems so.

ALISON: You told me he was.

SAM: Did I?

ALISON: But you didn't tell me Perry was gay.

SAM: I didn't know Perry was gay.

ALISON: Oh, Sam.

SAM: I didn't believe it.

ALISON: Oh, Sam.

SAM: I thought he could change.

ALISON: You thought I could change him.

SAM: Maybe.

ALISON: The Old Boy passes the ball to the Old Girl.

SAM: Oh, come on.

ALISON: Yes, well, I tried. I tried very hard.

SAM: Oh, Alison.

ALISON: And if I ultimately didn't succeed, at least I ended up in that golden land where the summer boys came from.

SAM: Otherwise known as Grosse Pointe.

ALISON: Exactly. Sometimes it's very gross, and sometimes there's no point, but I got what I wanted in the end.

(SAM *goes for another drink;* ALISON *holds out her glass.*)

Where are your manners?

SAM: Already?

ALISON: Why not?

(SAM *makes her another.*)

Gosh. I suppose this is what makes you such a good politician. You have a drink with people, and before long they're spilling the beans, and you've got them in your pocket.

SAM (*bringing her drink*): Pocket, hell. I'm trying to get you in my bed. (*He touches her hair.*)

ALISON: Hey! No fair! I've stripped down, I'm sitting here stark naked, and you're still buttoned to the nines! (*She kicks off her shoes.*)

SAM: What do you want to know?

ALISON: I'm not even sure. I've read so much about you. You were even in the magazine on the airplane, coming east. Harriet pointed it out to everyone in first class.

SAM: Oh, well, it's been mostly luck and pull.

ALISON: Don't be modest.

SAM: I'm serious. Mostly appointments, mostly through the Old Boy network. Kip Farraday, the guy from the Vineyard, got me my first job in the State Department, and I've been shunting around ever since.

ALISON: Aren't you running for governor in the fall?

SAM: If I'm nominated.

ALISON: Big step.

SAM: So they tell me. I'm trying to get cranked up for it.

ALISON: You don't want it?

SAM: I *want* to want it. That's about as far as it goes. Frankly, Alison, I have to say . . . I've been feeling a little . . . bankrupt lately. About what I do. I mean, I'm still writing the checks, but I'm not sure the money is there anymore.

ALISON: Sounds like you'll make a good governor.

SAM (*laughing*): Thanks.

(*They kiss.*)

ALISON (*finally breaking it off*): Hey! What about the lovely second wife, who sells condos in Washington and looked so trendy in *Vanity Fair*?

SAM: Ah. (*Pause.*) We're getting divorced. She's shoving off as soon as the political dust settles.

ALISON: Well, well.

SAM: It's tough being a politician's wife. I'm not always there, and when I am . . .

ALISON: You're not always there.

SAM: Exactly.

ALISON: Some rag I read in the supermarket called you a womanizer.

SAM: Whatever that means . . .

ALISON: It means you run around screwing women.

SAM: Hmmm.

ALISON: Do you?

SAM: Yes. Sometimes. Yes. Recently, too much so.

ALISON: Why?

SAM: Wish I knew.

ALISON: Sounds like you're going through your own explosion.

SAM: Maybe so.

ALISON: You and Perry. And me. All trying to make up for lost time.

(*Pause.*)

SAM: Let's make up for it right now. Come on. I'll rig the bedroom up like a sail locker.

ALISON: I think we're beyond the sail locker now.

SAM: I suppose we are.

ALISON: I think we've arrived at the Biltmore Hotel. Remember the Biltmore? The plan was to spend a fantastic night there before we went off to our colleges.

SAM: Okay. Let's pick up where we left off.

ALISON: God, you were the perfect gentleman. You took my arm and walked me there, after our big scene at the Whaler Bar. You checked me in. You stayed with me while I simmered down. You even lent me your handkerchief, which I still have. But like many gentlemen, you neglected to pay the bill.

SAM: Your bill was paid, Alison.

ALISON: Not by you, it wasn't.

SAM: Perry paid the bill.

ALISON: How do you know that?

SAM: And drove you up to college afterwards.

ALISON: How do you know that, Sam?

SAM: I asked him to.

ALISON: You *asked* him to?

SAM: I suggested it.

ALISON: I never knew that before.

SAM: You think I'd leave you stranded in some strange hotel?

ALISON: I always thought it was just luck, coming down in the morning, seeing Perry waiting in the lobby, under the clock. He never told me it was prearranged.

SAM: Because he was a gentleman, too.

ALISON: Of course! Dumb! Dumb me! I should have known! Both of you, gentlemen, all the way. You didn't want to dance with me anymore, so you got your friend to cut in.

SAM: I thought I was doing the right thing.

ALISON: Fuck the right thing!

SAM: Hey! Go easy.

ALISON: I'm suddenly feeling a little set up, Sam!

SAM: I think that is rather a bald way of—

ALISON: I'm beginning to feel you set up my whole damn *life*!

SAM: Oh, now hey, Alison.

ALISON: And never a call, to either of us, after you did it. Just a wedding present, card enclosed.

SAM: I thought it best not to interfere.

ALISON: Oh, sure. The under secretary of state sets up a puppet regime and then walks away from it. (*She goes to the bar.*)

SAM: Maybe you've had enough.

ALISON: Maybe I haven't. . . . Do you still think it was the right thing, knowing what you know now?

SAM: I think . . . I think we should terminate this little brush-up course in ancient history. We're not getting anywhere.

ALISON: I'm getting somewhere.

SAM: Oh, yes?

ALISON: You know why I came up here this weekend? I wanted to show you how well I've survived after all these years.

SAM: As indeed you have . . .

ALISON: I also wanted to go to bed with you and show you that little old Alison Shaeffer from the Clamshell still knows how to do it!

SAM: You might keep your voice down.

ALISON: But now I know I don't want that at all. All I want to hear is you say something along the lines of "I'm sorry."

SAM: I'm perfectly willing to say—

ALISON: No! You'll never say it! Not really! Not you! Not you and all the other old, old *boys* in your fucking *club*, moving your same dead old ideas around the backgammon board down in Washington!

SAM: I think you may have had too much to—

ALISON: Moving *people* around, too! Moving kids off to Vietnam and the Middle East and Lord knows where it'll be next! Moving *me* around, goddammit! Moving Perry! Oh, Christ, I thought I came to show you my shoes, but now I'd like to use them to brain you, you goddamn son of a bitch! (*She throws a shoe at him.*)

SAM (*backing off*): Hey, come on, please . . .

ALISON: Oh, hell. Don't worry. That wouldn't do any good, either. I'd never be able to bash my way through that thick shell you guys have built around yourselves all these years— no, wrong, all these *generations*! (*She finds her shoe, puts it back on.*) No wonder your wives give up, trying to break in! No wonder you fool around, trying to break out! Well, let me tell you something, Mr. Old Boy! *I'm* sorry! *Me!* I'm saying it to you. Know why? Because I don't think you've ever loved anyone. Love? You don't know the meaning of the word! You wouldn't know it if it stared you in the face!

(*She storms out. SAM stands staring after her. A hymn comes up: "Ten Thousand Times, Ten Thousand." Fade to black.*)

ACT TWO

The ringing of church bells. SAM, *looking disheveled, with rumpled hair, in his shirtsleeves, sits writing on a notepad, sipping coffee. After a moment, the sound of knocking.*

SAM (*calling out*): It's open!

(BUD *comes in, dressed as before. He carries his briefcase.*)

BUD: You look awful.

SAM: Thanks.

BUD: No, you do.

SAM: I didn't get much sleep last night.

BUD: Who does around here? Christ, between drunken parents arguing in the parking lot, and those fucking bells! . . . God-dammit, ding-dong!

SAM: The call to worship, Bud. In about a half an hour, we're going to stride manfully to the chapel, where for a rather long hour, we will thank Thee, Lord our God, with hearts, and hands, and voices. (*He returns to his work.*)

BUD (*glancing toward the bedroom*): All clear, by the way?

SAM: Of course it's all clear.

BUD: She left?

SAM: She didn't stay.

BUD: That's something new.

SAM: No comment. (*Again he returns to his work.*)

BUD: You really do look kind of beat, Sam.

SAM: I'll get fixed up.

BUD: I brought along some of that Pan-Cake they gave you on "MacNeil-Lehrer." Want me to get it?

SAM: Nope. (*He crumples up a paper.*)

BUD: What the hell are you doing?

SAM: Trying to figure out what to say.

BUD (*opens his folder*): I've said it. Right here. I'm quite proud of it, actually. After some passionate remarks about the need for new standards in American education, I modulate neatly into a discussion of public health, and wind up with a tender plea for human compassion.

SAM: You're a cynical bastard, Bud.

BUD: I like to win, Sam.

SAM: Think I'll do this one on my own, actually.

BUD: Yes? It doesn't look like you're getting very far.

SAM: I haven't, yet.

BUD: You've got twenty minutes before the schedule kicks in. (*Reading from his folder:*) Services in the chapel at ten. Coffee for special guests in the vestry at eleven-fifteen. Commencement exercises begin promptly at noon.

SAM: Then I'll wing it.

BUD: *Wing* it! You!

SAM: I've done it before.

BUD: Oh, sure. With the League of Women Voters?

SAM: That was okay. (*He starts off to get dressed.*)

BUD (*calling after him*): What? The Q and A was a ritual castration.

SAM: What about the Gridiron Club?

BUD: Oh, right. When you tried to be funny.

SAM: I *was* funny. I got a huge laugh.

BUD: That was a groan, Sam. A universal groan.

SAM: Anyway, this will be different. I know my audience better.

BUD: That's what scares me. You'll get all preppy and in-group, the way you were at that press conference.

SAM (*as he gets dressed*): You think so, Bud? Why? All I plan to do is open with a couple of sly, demeaning jokes about blacks and women. Then, after some comments about trust funds and deb parties, I'll slip into the main body of my speech, pleading passionately for lower capital gains taxes and higher-caliber handguns. I'll try to season these thoughts, of course, with vigorous, contemporary language: "Gosh," I'll say, and "What the dickens!" and even "Darn it all!" Toward the end, I'll toss in a few subtle anti-Semitisms, but gee whiz, Bud, most of those will be directed strictly against Israel. Finally, I'll refer to my old friend Perry, but I'll be so tight-assed and tongue-tied that it will only show that I'm totally out of touch with my own feelings.

BUD: You're kind of hyper today, aren't you?

SAM: Oh, yes I am, Bud. Yes I am. So hyper that when the ceremony is over, I plan to dash back here and change into my pink polo shirt and lime-green pants with little whales on them. Then, after too many martinis, and too few chicken sandwiches—on white bread, with the crusts cut off—I'll just drive recklessly off into the sunset in my green Volvo station wagon for an adulterous affair with the waitress at the local cocktail bar.

BUD: That last little detail has the ring of truth.

SAM: Oh, hell, Bud. Lighten up.

BUD: I'm thinking of your career, Sam.

SAM: And your own.

BUD: Sure my own. Katie called last night.

SAM: What else is new?

BUD: I'll tell you what's new. What's new is a new offer from my old law firm. Six figures. With a guaranteed partnership in three years. That's what's new.

SAM: What does Katie think?

BUD: She wants me home. The kids want me home. The dog wants me home.

SAM: What about the cat?

BUD: The cat can't make up its mind. . . . And neither can I, Sam. I said I'd decide today.

SAM: You mean you'd quit on me? Even before the convention?

BUD: I want to stay, Sam. Really! I want to go all the way to the top right by your side. There are some guys, they walk into a room, and you like them, you trust them, you could work for them easily all the days of your life! You're one of those guys, Sam. I sensed it when I met you, and the voters will sense it, too. You're our best shot in this weird world, and if you'll just keep your eye on the goddamn ball, you could be President one of these days!

SAM: And you think I'd mess that up if I said a few words about a dear, dead friend.

BUD: I think you might. Yes.

SAM: Well, I'm sorry. I have certain loyalties. . . .

BUD: Maybe it's time to stop playing Old Boy, Sam.

SAM: Maybe you're getting a little big for your britches, Bud.

BUD: Which is an Old Boy expression if I ever heard one.

SAM: Bug off, Bud.

BUD: Fuck you, Sam!

SAM: Watch the language, please!

BUD: "Fuck"? "Fuck" 's bad? We don't say it, we just do it, huh?

(DEXTER *comes in, now in Sunday clericals.*)

DEXTER: Behold, the bridegroom cometh!

SAM: Good morning, Dexter.

DEXTER: I'm here to conduct you to chapel.

SAM: You must think we need it.

DEXTER: Oh, I've walked in on worse in my thirty-odd years at the school.

BUD: I'll bet you have.

DEXTER (*to* SAM): I'm doing the sermon today. The rector has awarded me that privilege.

SAM (*as he ties his tie*): You obviously run the joint, Dexter. You should be rector yourself.

DEXTER: I put myself up for it, you know. During the last search. I proposed myself as an in-house candidate.

SAM: How'd you come out?

DEXTER: Fine, for a while. I was a finalist in the selection process. I had high hopes.

SAM: What happened? Why'd they pick that fatuous glad-hander over you?

DEXTER: Oh, well. You see, he was married. I wasn't. It came down to that.

SAM: Ah.

(*Pause.*)

BUD (*who has been looking out*): I notice a TV van out there.

DEXTER: Oh, yes. I meant to say.

BUD: You meant to say what?

DEXTER: Mrs. Pell wants some sense of the occasion.

BUD: I thought we agreed.

DEXTER: It's strictly local news. And the cameras will remain unobtrusively in the rear.

BUD: Which means they'll commandeer the front row. And go national if they can.

DEXTER: Oh, now. Let's be more charitable with our brethren of the press.

SAM: Let's at least go to church. . . . You coming, Bud?

BUD: I already hit early mass in town.

SAM: Go for the double feature.

BUD: No thanks.

SAM: Come on. It's a gorgeous service. The rich, compelling language of the *Book of Common Prayer* . . . "We have left undone those things which we ought to have done. And we have done those things which we ought not to have done. And there is no health in us."

DEXTER: Good for you, Sam. Letter-perfect.

BUD: It's a great sound bite, Sam. You could base your campaign on it.

SAM: Go back to bed, Bud.

BUD: I'm awake, man! You're the one who's asleep.

(*He goes out.*)

DEXTER: What an insistent young man.

SAM: He'll go far.

DEXTER: I envy the Catholics. They see things so clearly. Martin Luther made it all much more difficult when he put us in charge of our own salvation.

(*More church bells.*)

Well. We should go.

SAM: Lead, kindly light.

(*He goes into the bedroom for his jacket.*)

DEXTER: You might be interested to know that I'm speaking today on St. Paul.

SAM (*from bedroom*): Hey! My buddy!

DEXTER: Yes. I dug up the sermon I gave the year you graduated. I explore how Paul moves beyond the erotic to a larger kind of love.

SAM: Sounds like just my meat.

(*They go off, as* HARRIET *comes on, followed by* PERRY. *She is dressed for graduation. He wears a senior blazer and slacks and carries a sports trophy with a tennis player mounted on top.*)

HARRIET: There he goes! Cut him loose from the herd!

PERRY (*calling out*): Sam! Hey, Sam!

(SAM *comes on, now in his graduation blazer.*)

Mother wants to see you.

SAM (*hugging him, indicating the trophy*): Congratulations, man! The tennis trophy! What did I tell ya?

PERRY: Where's your Leadership Cup?

SAM: I left it with my father. He wants it for mixing martinis.

HARRIET: Hail to the chief who in triumph advances. (*She shakes* SAM's *hand.*) I simply want to congratulate you, Sam, for walking off with every prize in the school.

PERRY: Except the tennis trophy, Mother.

HARRIET: Oh, well, that was a foregone conclusion.

PERRY: I wish I'd won the Drama Cup.

HARRIET: I'm delighted you didn't, darling. (*To* SAM:) Now, Sam: what new worlds will you conquer next?

SAM: Princeton, I hope.

HARRIET: You hope? Aren't you sure?

SAM: My father's had some setbacks lately. We had to apply for a scholarship. If I don't get it, I'll end up at State.

HARRIET: Surely it's time to pull a few strings.

SAM: Those strings are getting a little frayed these days.

HARRIET: I wish you could join Perry at Middlebury.

PERRY: I wish I'd gotten into Columbia.

HARRIET: Nonsense. Middlebury is the perfect solution. They have skiing, they have square dancing. . . .

SAM: They have girls.

HARRIET: Exactly, Sam. They are coeducational. Which means hundreds of lovely girls, all there waiting to be kissed. . . .

PERRY: Maybe they're there for other reasons, Mother.

HARRIET: Maybe they are. . . . Now, Perry, dear, I wonder if you'd go stand in that line, and get us one of those delicious-looking fruit punches on this hot June day?

SAM: I'll do it.

HARRIET: No, I want Perry to do it. Would you, dear? For your mother and your Old Boy?

PERRY (*saluting*): Aye, aye, sir.

(*He goes off.*)

HARRIET (*watching him go*): That, Sam, is your doing.

SAM: What?

HARRIET: That. The whole thing. The tennis prize, Middle-bury, the confident way he walks. I put it all down to you, Sam. You've been a marvelous Old Boy.

SAM: That was just the first year, Mrs. Pell. Now he's one of my best friends.

HARRIET: There are friends and there are friends, Sam.

SAM: No. I'm serious. We would've roomed together this year, except I can't stand the *Forza del Destino*.

HARRIET: It's that *Forza* thing we've still got to fight, Sam. All the way to the finish.

SAM: Excuse me?

HARRIET: Tell me. What are your plans for the summer, Sam?

SAM: Teaching sailing, actually.

HARRIET: Teaching *sailing*!

SAM: On the Vineyard.

HARRIET: On Martha's Vineyard! What fun.

SAM: I visited there last summer, and this summer I got the sailing job at the Yacht Club.

HARRIET: How enterprising, Sam.

SAM: It's a job, anyway. And I like it there.

HARRIET: Perry wants to spend his summer in New York.

SAM: So he said.

HARRIET: He says if he can't go to Columbia, he can still do that.

SAM: Sounds fair to me.

HARRIET: Taking some stupid course on medieval music.

SAM: He loves music.

HARRIET: It does not seem like a terribly healthy summer to me, sitting around that hot, dirty city, listening to monks sing madrigals.

SAM: It's what he wants.

HARRIET: Of course, his father's there. Who now claims to be a photographer. And lives with an Italian woman half his age. And hardly gives Perry the time of day.

SAM: Perry likes him, though.

HARRIET: I know. (*Pause.*) It's hard not to. (*Pause.*) Sam, have you ever been out west?

SAM: No.

HARRIET: Would you like to go?

SAM: Of course.

HARRIET: All right now, Sam. Here's the thing. I would like it very much if you took Perry on a good, long trip out west this summer.

SAM: Oh, I couldn't—

HARRIET: No, now wait. I will give you the Buick station wagon, and carte blanche financially. My aunt Esther has a ranch in Montana and you can stop there for as long as you want. You can fish, you can ride, you can even work if you feel like it. Or you can move on. You can go to Nevada and gamble. You can go to Wyoming and visit the brothels. You can end up in Hollywood, I don't care, just as long as you go. I think it will be good for you. I know it will be good for Perry.

SAM: Wow!

HARRIET: There you are.

SAM: Except I've already got this job.

HARRIET: I should imagine, Sam, that there are twenty other boys who would give their eyeteeth to teach sailing on Martha's Vineyard.

SAM: There's another thing, though.

HARRIET: What other thing?

SAM: I've got this girl, Mrs. Pell.

HARRIET: Ah. The Girl.

SAM: We're kind of going together.

HARRIET: Yes. Perry told me about the Girl.

SAM: She's the real reason I got the job down there.

HARRIET: Ah, yes. Now let's see if I've got the facts straight. You met her there last summer, and her father owns a hardware store, and she came up to some dance.

SAM: Right.

HARRIET: Perry said he treated you both to dinner at the inn. He said she was very attractive.

SAM: She thought Perry was terrific.

HARRIET: And I'm sure she thinks you're *more* than terrific.

SAM: We get along.

HARRIET: Well, then she'll keep.

SAM: Keep?

HARRIET: While you go west.

SAM: Could I bring her along?

HARRIET: No, Sam. That might be a little tricky.

SAM: Then I don't know. . . .

HARRIET: I'll tell you something else, Sam. There need be no more difficulty about Princeton. I know a man on the board of trustees, and I'll sing him your praises.

SAM: What if Perry doesn't want to go west?

HARRIET: He'll go, if you go.

(*Pause.* SAM *thinks.*)

SAM: This is a tough one, Mrs. Pell.

HARRIET: It's the tough ones that are worth winning, Sam.

SAM: Okay. I'll do it.

HARRIET: Would you, Sam? That is princely of you. Princely. Of a Princeton man. . . . Now I want to meet your parents. I want to tell them they've produced a prince among men.

SAM: Just my father's here. My stepmother couldn't make it.

HARRIET: Oh, dear. Not ill, I hope.

SAM: Oh, no. She's down south, marching for civil rights.

HARRIET: What fun. Well, then I'll tell your *father* he's produced a prince among men.

SAM: He won't agree.

HARRIET: What? Doesn't he appreciate you?

SAM: He thinks I could stand some improvement.

HARRIET (*taking his arm*): Oh, well, all parents think that about their children.

(*They go off, as* PERRY *comes out in khakis and a flannel shirt. He shouts for* SAM *a number of times, as if they were in a great open space. Then he goes to the bench and honks the "horn" as if it were a car.*)

PERRY (*calling off*): Come on! We haven't got all day!

(*He honks again. Other car sounds are heard passing, as if he were parked along a highway. Finally* SAM *enters, now in a pullover shirt.*)

   Where the hell have you been?

SAM: I was talking to those babes we met on the trail.

PERRY: I've been waiting for half an hour.

SAM: They want to party.

PERRY: Can't.

SAM: They have beer.

PERRY: Can't, Sam. Have to make Sacramento by four tomorrow.

SAM: They have beer, they have burgers.

PERRY: We've got to sell the car and make a four o'clock plane. Now get the hell *in*.

SAM (*looking over his shoulder*): We could catch another plane. There are plenty of planes. You think there's just one plane?

PERRY: I've got to make freshman week.

SAM: What's freshman week? That's for high school guys. You're beyond that shit, Perry. You're a big boy now.

PERRY: In, Sam. Please.

(SAM *reluctantly gets in the car.* PERRY *starts to turn the key.* SAM *grabs his hand.*)

SAM: The dark-haired one thought you were cute, Perry.

PERRY: She did not.

SAM: She did. She said, "Where's your cute friend?"

PERRY: She didn't say that.

SAM: She said, "Where's your cute friend? I want to open my throbbing loins to him, tonight, under the western stars."

PERRY (*starting the car; they jerk forward*): Bullshit.

(*They drive.*)

SAM: So where will we camp tonight then?

PERRY: On the way somewhere.

SAM: What'll we do? Toast marshmallows? Tell ghost stories?

PERRY: Jesus, Sam. There's such a thing as making conversation.

SAM (*looking back*): Okay. I'll begin. Seen any good-looking girls lately?

PERRY: Very funny.

(*They drive.*)

I keep thinking about next year.

SAM: I keep thinking about back there.

PERRY: I'll bet we don't connect much next year. Different colleges, different friends. I'll bet we don't see each other much anymore.

SAM (*mock sentimental*): "I'll be seeing you, in all the old familiar places . . ."

(*He turns on the "radio." We hear classical music. He finds a ball game. At an exciting moment, PERRY turns it off.*)

Hey! Come on!

PERRY: You really piss me off sometimes, Sam. You know that?

SAM: Yeah, well, don't get so corny, then.

PERRY: Just because I have feelings, I'm corny. Just because I value our friendship, I'm now corny.

SAM: Change the channel, Perry.

PERRY: Sometimes I think you're a cold son of a bitch, Sam. You really are a cold, thoughtless guy sometimes.

SAM: Oooh. Ouch. What brought that on?

PERRY: You leave me standing there while you shoot the breeze with a couple of babes. You always have to listen to the fucking Red Sox, but when an opera comes on, we have to turn it right off. . . .

SAM: Oh, for chrissake . . .

PERRY: And when we were at the ranch, you kept going after that waitress. . . .

SAM: What's wrong with that?

PERRY: You didn't even *like* her. You *said* you didn't like her. And yet you screwed her, you son of a bitch.

SAM: So what if I did?

PERRY: You never even told her goodbye.

SAM: That was an oversight.

PERRY: That was shitty, Sam. That was shitty behavior.

SAM: Just because you . . .

PERRY: Because I what?

SAM: Don't care about girls.

PERRY: I care about girls. I cared about *that* girl. I cared about her more than you did.

SAM: Then why don't you care about those girls back *there*? Why, during this whole trip, whenever there's a chance to go out with girls, you're always backing off, for chrissake?

PERRY: Bullshit, Sam. Apply the bullshit quotient, please.

SAM: You're always backing off. I mean, when we were in Reno, and had that chance to go to that cathouse, you wanted to go to *Lawrence of Arabia*! I mean, what are you? A fag, or what?

(PERRY *jams on the brakes; both lurch forward.*)

PERRY: I'm not a fag, Sam.

SAM: Those girls are just *sitting* there, waiting for us to make our *move*!

PERRY: I'm not a fag.

SAM: Well, I mean, you've got your problems, Perry.

PERRY (*hitting him on the arm*): I'm not a fag.

SAM (*hitting him back*): Hey! Knock it off!

PERRY: Get out of the car!

SAM: Says who?

PERRY: Me! Get out of my goddamn car, Sam!

SAM (*getting out*): Okay. Fine. I'll go back and see those girls! (*Through the "window":*) So long, fag.

PERRY (*jumping out of the car*): Don't call me that.

SAM (*going off*): Fag! Fag! Fairy Perry!

PERRY (*leaping on him*): Go fuck yourself, Sam! Go fuck yourself!

(*They fight. SAM is stronger. He ultimately gets on top.*)

SAM: Or should I fuck *you*, Perry? Want your Old Boy to fuck you? Huh? Huh? (*He plants a big kiss on PERRY's lips.*) How's that? Is that what you want?

(PERRY *rolls free. They both get up, separate. Sounds of traffic going by are heard periodically.*)

PERRY: I'm not a fag, Sam!

SAM: Okay, okay. I'm sorry.

PERRY: I don't know what I am. But I'm not that.

SAM: Okay, okay. (*Pause.*) I think the trouble with us, the trouble with both of us, is we just need more sex. Men don't get sex, they get frustrated, and fight among themselves. It happens with rats. (*Pause.*) Now here we are out west the summer before we go to college, and you're constantly bringing me down as far as girls are concerned, and so naturally I just blew up.

PERRY: Just leave it, Sam, okay?

SAM: I mean, that's why I thought you should see those babes. Our last chance out here, and I thought you should have a sexual experience. That's all I thought, and I'll bet your mother would agree with me.

PERRY: I've had a sexual experience.

SAM: Yeah, yeah.

PERRY: Okay. Don't believe me then.

SAM: When?

PERRY: That's my business.

SAM: Not this summer, that's for sure.

PERRY: Last summer, if you must know. While you were having yours.

SAM: When you went to New York?

PERRY: Right.

SAM: Do I know her?

PERRY: No.

SAM: Did you get in?

PERRY: No.

SAM: But you came close?

PERRY: Maybe.

SAM: Where'd you meet her?

PERRY: At a friend's.

SAM: What friend?

PERRY: We met at my father's.

SAM: She was a friend of your father's?

PERRY: Right.

SAM: Oh, my God! An older woman! Did she show you the ropes? Remember *Room at the Top*?

PERRY: Yes.

SAM: Jesus. Sneaky Pete here. Last summer he's learning the ropes from Simone Signoret! How come you didn't tell me?

PERRY: I don't have to tell you everything.

SAM: Thought I'd tease you about it?

PERRY: Maybe.

SAM: You like her, don't you? That's why you turned down those babes. You like her. I can tell.

PERRY: It's not a her, Sam.

SAM: Not a her?

PERRY: I was sleeping on the couch over at my father's, and this friend of his got in bed with me.

SAM: Jesus! Did you kick him out?

PERRY: Sure. Oh, sure. That's what I did. Immediately.

SAM: You told your dad, I hope.

PERRY: No.

SAM: My dad would've gone through the *roof*!

PERRY: My dad's kind of loose about things, actually.

SAM: But God! It must've been *gross*! Did he touch your dong?

PERRY: No. Of course not. No.

SAM: So. Ho-hum. Big deal. What are you? Scarred for life? That make you scarred for life?

PERRY: No.

SAM: Okay. Then it's water over the dam.

PERRY: It's not over the dam yet.

SAM: What? He's still bothering you?

PERRY: Not bothering me.

SAM: Whatever you call it, there are laws against it, Perry.

PERRY: Are there laws against going to plays?

SAM: What are you talking about?

PERRY: Remember when I got special permission from school to see the Royal Shakespeare? This guy got the tickets.

SAM: Jesus. And you went!

PERRY: I wanted to see the play.

SAM: You are grossing me out here, Perry. You are definitely grossing me out. Did you have a sexual encounter?

PERRY: I don't want to talk about it.

SAM: You did, didn't you? You had a sexual encounter with this guy.

PERRY: All right. I did.

SAM: Oh my God! This is total gross-out time!

PERRY: Well, you might as well know I'm meeting him in New York tomorrow night!

SAM: Is that why you wanted to get back?

PERRY: Yes!

SAM: Oh my God.

PERRY: I like him, Sam. I like him more than you ever liked that waitress at the ranch.

SAM: I can't believe I'm hearing this.

PERRY: Yeah, well, he wants me to come down from Middlebury and see him this fall, and stay at his place, and go to the opera with him, too, if I want to!

SAM: And you want to?

PERRY: I don't know what I want.

SAM: Get in the car. Get in the *car*, Perry! My turn to drive.

(*They get back in the car;* SAM *drives.*)

You were right, what you said back there, Perry. About maybe not seeing each other much after this. . . . Because I have to tell you, Perry, if you start hanging out with guys like that, and going to the opera all the time, if that's what you want, then count me out.

PERRY: I'm not sure I want that.

SAM: Well, I know what I want. I want to walk into a room with a pretty girl on my arm, and know that she's mine for the evening. I want to get married someday, and have great sex three times a night, and even during the day. I want to have kids, and dogs, and play sports on weekends, and be a

respected leader in my community. I want to move on up
and contribute something positive to my country and the
world. Maybe you think that's bullshit, but that's what I want.

PERRY: I want that, too. You think I don't want that? I want
that every minute of the day. I see a guy getting cozy with a
girl, I envy him. I see a baby carriage, I think that's never for
me. I see a house, just some dumb *house* for shit's sake, and I
wonder if I'll ever live in one, and who would ever live there
with me.

SAM: Oh, come on.

PERRY: It's true, Sam. . . . And at night, I have these feelings
. . . these other feelings . . . these strong feelings . . . about
guys . . . sometimes even about you, Sam . . .

SAM: Me? Jesus, Perry . . . What—do you have us doing?

PERRY: We—make love.

SAM: Am I any good?

PERRY: I'm serious, Sam!

SAM: I know. Go on.

PERRY: I have these feelings. And I pray, I *pray*—I don't believe
in any of that horseshit—but I pray to God that He will take
. . . that He will *burn* these feelings out of me forever and
ever, and send me some *girl*, and we'll fall in love, and live
happily ever after.

SAM: I know a girl who likes you a lot.

PERRY: Yeah? Who?

SAM: Alison.

PERRY: Alison?

SAM: She likes you a lot. (*Pause.*) Do you like her?

PERRY: Of course.

SAM: You sure said you did when I brought her up to school.

PERRY: I like her a lot.

SAM: Take her out if you want.

PERRY: Take Alison out?

SAM: You'd be a great pair.

PERRY: I thought you liked her.

SAM: My father wants me to cool it.

PERRY: But she likes *you.*

SAM: She thinks you're a fascinating guy.

PERRY: She thinks I'm a big spender.

SAM: "A fascinating guy." Those were her exact words.

PERRY: She said that?

SAM: I swear. Now think positively. Take your sexual desires and refocus them on Alison.

PERRY: I thought she was your girl.

SAM: I'm not ready for a steady relationship.

PERRY: That's for sure.

SAM: Actually, you'd be getting me off the hook.

PERRY: We got along, didn't we? Alison and me. That time.

SAM: I couldn't get a word in edgewise.

PERRY: I told her we were kindred spirits.

SAM: There you are. Kindred spirits. Hey, suppose I fix you up with her? I'm seeing her in New York next week. I'll work something out. Meanwhile, you tell your faggy friend to bug off. . . .

PERRY: I'll say I've got a previous engagement.

SAM: Okay. Say that. And hey! Alison's going to the University of Vermont this fall. You could drive over from Middlebury in that new Corvette your mother promised you. She loves Corvettes. She told me. You'll snow the pants off her. So see? It's perfect! Your prayers are answered, Buddy!

PERRY: Right.

SAM: So. We are no longer doooomed to hang around bars with creeps in New York, and listen to the Farts of Destiny. We're rejoining the human race. Is it a deal?

PERRY: It's a deal, Sam. It's a real deal.

SAM (*pulling over*): Fine. Now let's pull over and take a good manly pee. Those beers with those babes have caught up with me.

(SAM *stops the car. They exit. Traffic sounds are heard, then drowned out by: A hymn: "For the Beauty of the Earth."*)
    (ALISON *comes on, holding a cup of coffee; she looks around. The hymn fades as* HARRIET *enters.*)

HARRIET: What are you doing out here?

ALISON: Getting a little fresh air.

HARRIET: Alison, dear, I'm not sure it's a good idea to be stalking around, in front of all these students, with a cup of coffee in your hand. You look a little . . . disconnected. Come back into the vestry.

ALISON: No thanks.

HARRIET: Then I wonder if you might tell me what in heaven's name is the matter. You've contradicted me all weekend. I thought we were a solid front, you and I. Do you think our dear Perry would be happy if he knew his mother and his wife had suddenly started bickering in public?

ALISON: I'm not sure.

HARRIET: Well, *I'm* sure of several things, Alison. I'm sure that life will be much pleasanter for both of us if we don't argue. I'm sure that those handsome checks which land on your doorstep every Christmas are not based on your being disagreeable. I'm sure that my grandson's future is at least somewhat dependent on you and I pulling together.

(*She sees* SAM, *who enters, now dressed in his suit.*)

Ah, dear Sam! Come inside before the graduation march. We're having coffee and rolls.

ALISON: The coffee's weak, the rolls are repulsive.

HARRIET: Alison—I think you and I should probably continue our own conversation on the trip back down to the real world.

(*She takes* ALISON's *cup and goes.*)

ALISON (*to* SAM): I've been waiting to waylay you.

SAM: Uh-oh. Do you plan to keep your shoes on?

ALISON: I'll try. . . . Are you all right, by the way?

SAM: I think so.

ALISON: I was watching you all during chapel. You just sat and stared. And then disappeared.

SAM: I took a walk around the pond.

ALISON: Thinking about your speech?

SAM: Thinking about lots of things. I was a manipulative bastard, wasn't I?

ALISON: Oh, hell, I made my own bed, too. Though I didn't get much sleep in it last night.

SAM: I wish I could make things up to you.

ALISON: You can, actually. That's why I'm waylaying you. I wonder if you could get me a job.

SAM: A job?

ALISON: Through your Old Boy network. I can't live this way any longer. I want to earn my own keep. Which means a job. I suppose I could slink back to the Clamshell, but I like to think I've grown beyond it.

SAM: Let's see . . . who do I know in the shoe business?

ALISON: No, I'm serious. I can't type, or work a computer, or do any of those things. But I'm smart. And still ambitious.

SAM: I'll check around.

ALISON: I'd be wonderful in the State Department. After all, I've maintained a diplomatic front for over half my life.

SAM: Until last night.

ALISON: Lookit, I've been in analysis long enough to know that you don't get mad at people unless you feel pretty strongly about them.

SAM: I'll buy that.

ALISON: So. Suppose we work it this way. You find me a job, any job, anywhere, and we'll forgive and forget. Or rather remember—the good things. There's something between us, Sam. There was on the Vineyard, and there was in your room last night. We might even see each other occasionally. . . . (*Pause.*) I mean, if I worked in Washington . . . (*Pause.*) Or even if I didn't. (*Pause.*) Oh, Lord. Now I feel I'm back at the Whaler Bar, pleading for your attention.

SAM: I'll try to find you a job, Alison.

ALISON: Thank you.

SAM: But I can't see you again.

ALISON: Why not?

SAM: Perry.

ALISON: Perry's dead now.

SAM: So am I.

(HARRIET, DEXTER, *and* BUD *join them.* DEXTER *wears an academic robe, and carries another, along with a purple hood. They all talk almost at once.*)

DEXTER: Allrightee! Time to gird up our loins! (*He begins to drape* SAM *with an academic robe.*)

BUD (*to* SAM): What did I tell you? That TV crowd has moved right in.

HARRIET: Sam, dear, when you mention the tennis court, say I'm thinking of a clay surface. It gives a truer bounce. Be sure you mention clay.

DEXTER (*fussing with the robes*): "Hath not the potter power over the clay?" Paul. Romans. Nine, twenty-one.

ALISON (*low, to* SAM): Are you sure you're all right?

DEXTER (*adjusting a purple hood*): We couldn't decide which of your honorary degrees to reflect in your hood, the purple from Williams or the blue from Yale.

BUD (*handing* SAM *a stack of note cards*): You can fall back on these if you get into trouble.

DEXTER (*adjusting the hood*): We finally chose Williams. The imperial purple seemed particularly appropriate.

SAM: Dexter, did Paul say "The truth shall set thee free"?

DEXTER (*as he fusses with the robes*): No, that was Christ. In the Fourth Gospel. Why?

SAM: I can't get it out of my head.

(*A trumpet fanfare is heard.*)

DEXTER: Ah, the trumpet soundeth. . . . Mrs. Pell, if you would stand over there, behind the class marshal . . .

HARRIET: Absolutely.

(HARRIET *goes off.*)

DEXTER: And Mrs. Pell, Jr., if you would stand beside her . . .

ALISON: All right.

(ALISON *goes off.* DEXTER *turns to* BUD.)

DEXTER: And you, sir, have a reserved seat out in front.

BUD: Right. I see it. Out by the parking lot.

(BUD *goes off the opposite side. The lights focus in on* SAM *and* DEXTER, *now center.*)

DEXTER: And now, Sam, what will happen is that we'll march over to the dais, and then we'll have the prayers, and the hymn, and the handing out of diplomas, and then the awarding of the prizes, and then the rector will make the introduction, and you'll speak. It's as simple as that.

(DEXTER *is out by now.* SAM *is alone on stage, as if on the speaker's platform.*)

SAM: Thank you, Dr. Fayerweather . . . (*Carefully:*) Members of the faculty . . . members of the graduating class . . . students . . . parents . . . distinguished guests . . . babies . . . golden retrievers . . . and squirrels. (*Pause. He glances at Bud's notes, then rejects them, tucking them away in his jacket.*) When I was a boy here, we were always looking for the right answers. Sometimes they were in the back of the algebra book: "If A works twice as hard as B," and so forth, and the answer would always be some neat, round number, like four, and it was our job to show how we arrived at it. And at the end of the school year, we'd take exams, and neatly circle all our answers, fold our blue books, and sign the pledge on the outside: "I pledge my honor as a gentleman that I have neither given nor received help." (*Pause.*) We also found answers at home, when we returned for vacation. "If I go out on a date, what time do I have to be home?" The answer was twelve. "What's wrong with communism?" It's evil. "What must I do to earn your love and respect?" Work twice as hard as B. Always there were answers. And if neither the school nor our family could provide them, we still assumed they were there, somewhere

on down the line, at Harvard, in Washington, or in Heaven.
(*Pause.*) Today we're lucky if we find the right questions.
Maybe that's all a good school can do these days—teach us
good questions. At least, since I've been back, it's taught me
to ask a few. And maybe now it's time for me to take an exam
on them. After all, as Mr. MacDonald over there used to say
in classy civ, "the unexamined life is not worth living." Okay?
So here's my final exam. (*Pause.*) First question. Big question.
Huge subject. Love in the Western world. What in God's
name is our problem? Why do we worry so much about un-
conventional forms of love? Are we afraid of love? Are we
threatened by it when it stands out from the crowd? Here at
school, we studied those long, bloody wars fought over religion. This country was founded as a haven from these wars.
If we so cherish religious tolerance, why not sexual tolerance
as well? Will there be a time when people's sexual natures are
considered matters for their own soul, like their religion? Answer: let's hope. (*Pause.*) Next question. What about the AIDS
epidemic? Is this the result of sexual freedom, or sexual re-
pression? By maligning gay people, any group of people, have
we caused them to turn in on themselves in self-destructive
ways? And by doing this, by creating these ghettoes, have we
ghettoized ourselves, cutting ourselves off from the rich diversity which constitutes American life? I can see Mr. Burn-
ham writing in the margin: "Interesting, if true." (*Pause.*)
Main question. Is there something in my own life which re-
lates to all this? Yes. Oh, yes. I can answer this one. When I
was a boy here, I had a friend—a good friend—a gay friend
—whom I persuaded to conform to a conventional life. Why?
Was it natural? No. It was unnatural, to him. Was it right?
No. It was wrong for him. Why did I do it, then? Was it
something in me—some attempt to deny some passion in my
own soul? Mr. Montgomery might add this comment: "Try
to avoid clichés." (*Pause.*) Final question. What happened to

this boy? He died. Why did he die? From a desperate attempt
to make up for lost time. Who is responsible for that? Me. I
am responsible. I was his Old Boy. I had a special obligation.
(*Pause.*) "Bullshit," Perry might say. "Apply the bullshit quotient immediately." But I don't think I'm bullshitting now.
. . . (*Pause.*) Optional question. Extra credit. What can I do
about this? Nothing. Can I bring him back? No. Can I apologize to him? No. Too late, too late, too late. What then?
. . . Oh, Perry, why do I discover this now, only now, when
there's nothing to do, nothing to be done . . . when I can
never tell you . . . never say . . . never even . . . (*He stops,
looks around.*) I pledge my honor as a gentleman that I have
neither given nor received . . . Oh, God.

(*He covers his face with his hands. Then* DEXTER *appears solicitously,
speaks to the audience.*)

DEXTER: Perhaps we might conclude the ceremonies with
another hymn. (*Calling off:*) Would you start us off, Mr.
Benbow? (*Starts singing, leading:*) "Faith of our fathers, holy
faith. . . ."

(*He puts an arm around* SAM *and helps him from the stage as the music
and singing come up.*)
　　(BUD *enters, dials the telephone.*)

BUD: Hi. Looks like I'll be home for dinner. . . . Oh, sure. We'll
be out of here fast. . . . Because he booted the ball, baby. I'll
tell you when I get there. . . .

(*Knocking is heard offstage.*)

Someone's at the door. . . . We'll talk when I get home. . . .
Hey. Keep the kids up, will you? Haven't seen them in cen-

turies. . . . Love you, too. . . . (*Hangs up; calls out:*) Yo! It's open.

(HARRIET *comes in.*)

HARRIET: I'd like to speak to your lord and master.

BUD: He's taking a shower.

HARRIET: Well, I'm leaving. I wonder if you'd give him a message.

BUD: Shoot.

HARRIET: Tell him, if you would, that I have fought all my life against what is soft and sick and self-indulgent.

BUD: Okay.

HARRIET: Tell him that I left my husband, and raised my son, and hope to raise my grandson in the belief that there are such things as traditional values, decent behavior, and basic self-control.

BUD: Okay.

HARRIET (*starts out, then turns*): You might also tell him that he's broken my heart.

(*She goes, as we hear the sound of a shower and* SAM *singing.*)

SAM'S VOICE:

> "Fling out the banner! Let it ride,
> Skyward and seaward, high and wide!"

(DEXTER *comes out from within.*)

BUD: How's he doing?

DEXTER: Him that hath ears, let him hear. . . . Perhaps you'd like to stay while I investigate the extent of the damage.

BUD: Sure.

(DEXTER *goes off.* SAM *comes out in a terry-cloth robe, toweling his hair. He crosses to get the Bible by the telephone.*)

SAM: Where've you been?

BUD: Right here. Calling Katie.

SAM: Told her you'll take the new job, right?

BUD: Not yet.

SAM: Ah.

(*Crossing back, he flashes at* BUD *and exits.*)

BUD: You okay?

SAM (*reentering*): Never better. It's weird.

(*Exits again.*)

BUD: Feel like talking shop?

SAM (*now offstage*): Sure. While I get dressed.

BUD (*speaking toward offstage*): Okay, here goes. I'm not worried about the local news. That won't matter much. Tomorrow, when it goes nationwide, that's when the trouble starts. . . . "Well-bred"—or will they say "white-bread"?—"guberna-torial candidate delivers bizarre, highly emotional diatribe on gay rights at posh New England prep school." Not to mention the visual thing.

(SAM *comes out in khakis and an informal shirt, carrying a Val-Pac and a windbreaker.*)

SAM: The visual thing?

BUD: That moment at the end when you pulled your Muskie. . . .

SAM: I never touched my muskie.

BUD: *Senator* Muskie, Sam. New Hampshire, seventy-two. He cried. It cost him the primary. They called it "womanish behavior."

SAM (*putting on his shoes*): Maybe it got me the women's vote.

BUD: It got you the gay vote, Sam. If that. . . . The President will be very kind, of course. He'll give you a sad smile, and ask you to transfer to the Department of Health and Human Services.

SAM: I'll quit before he gets around to it.

BUD: Okay. So I'll call party headquarters and say you're withdrawing. For personal reasons.

SAM: Withdrawing?

BUD: You don't still plan to go for it?

SAM: Sure. What's the problem?

BUD: Here's the problem, Sam. The media will say—carefully, of course, to avoid a libel suit—that you're gay as a goose.

SAM: They said that about St. Paul.

BUD: Christ, Sam.

SAM: And about Him, too.

BUD: Watch it, pal.

SAM: You wait, Bud. They'll say it about you.

BUD: Fuck you, Sam.

SAM: Fuck you, Bud.

(DEXTER *comes in*.)

DEXTER: I keep walking in on the same scintillating exchange.

SAM: I've just discovered the pleasure of saying four-letter words.

DEXTER: It's a limited pleasure, and soon will pale. I've come to say a more significant word. Namely, goodbye.

SAM (*shaking hands*): So long, Dexter. I hope my speech didn't thoroughly disappoint you.

DEXTER: Well, I have to say that Mrs. Pell is giving her tennis court to Andover. And the rector is thinking of removing your name from the list of distinguished alumni.

SAM: Yippee! That makes it official! I'm no longer an Old Boy!

DEXTER: As for me . . . if you want my opinion . . . (*Pause.*) I was very moved by what you said. (*Pause.*) It made me wonder if once upon a time, I should have . . . (*Pause.*) But no. This is a good school, and I hope I've helped make it a better one.

SAM (*embracing him*): You have, Dexter. You have indeed.

(ALISON *enters*.)

ALISON: Well, what d'ya know?

SAM: What?

ALISON: "What." The man says "what." (*To* DEXTER *and* BUD:) Here is a man I thought was buttoned up for life. I told him so, last night, right here in this room. And now, today, he's suddenly turning himself inside out and upside down in front of all America. (*To* SAM:) That's what. You were great, sir.

SAM: You might have a slight disagreement about that with your mother-in-law.

ALISON: Already did. She wanted me to deny everything you said, or she'd cut me off without a cent.

SAM: What did you say?

ALISON: Never mind, but she left without me.

SAM: Then you need a ride.

ALISON: I've already found one. I ran into some folks who have room in their backseat of their green Volvo station wagon. They're headed in the general direction of my son's school. I'll stop there. Or rather start there . . . (*She starts out.*)

SAM: Alison. I don't know how much clout I'll have now, but I owe you a job.

ALISON: I'll remember that. I'll also remember your speech for a long, long time. Thank you.

(*She goes.* DEXTER *gets himself a glass of wine.*)

SAM: Well, come on, Bud. Let's go.

BUD: What makes you think I'm going with you, Sam?

SAM: Because you love me. You admitted it yesterday.

BUD: I also admitted yesterday I work for winners. I see a loser here.

SAM: You need a ride back down, man.

BUD: I imagine, knowing this school, there's a chartered bus headed straight for Grand Central.

DEXTER: I'm afraid there is.

SAM: That's dumb, Bud.

BUD: Ten minutes in a car with you, you'd con me out of that new job and back onto your staff.

SAM: I'd sure try.

(*A hymn is heard softly: "I Heard the Sound of Voices."*)

Well, I'm off, then. (*Hugs* BUD.) I'll miss you, Buddy. (*He starts out.*)

BUD: Sam! You could at least tell me what your plans are.

SAM: I thought I'd stick my thumb up my ass and go on faith.

BUD: That's a compelling agenda for the nineties, Sam.

DEXTER: And a rather lonely notion, besides.

SAM: I got it from Paul.

(*He goes.*)

DEXTER (*to* BUD): That's not Paul. And he shouldn't say that it is.

BUD: He was kidding. (*He looks after* SAM.) I think.

(*He goes.* DEXTER *salutes them with his wine as the music comes up and the lights dim.*)

PLUME

CENTER STAGE

☐ **TWELVE PLAYS by Joyce Carol Oates.** Innovative and intense, the drama of Joyce Carol Oates is as unique as her unmistakable voice, which can be clearly heard in each work's dialogue, soliloquy, or chorus. The twelve superb plays collected here incorporate specific issues of our time, from AIDS to racism, yet they go beyond current topics to intimately explore universal themes such as aging, death, and hope.   (267013—$14.95)

☐ **SHADOWLANDS by William Nicholson.** This extraordinary play based on the true story of the British philosopher and highly successful author of children's fantasies, C.S. Lewis, brilliantly portrays how love profoundly alters the idealistic philosopher—more than any teacher, book, or thought had before. "Engrossing, entertaining . . . literate, well-crafted, and discreetly brilliant." —Clive Barnes, *New York Post*   (267323—$7.95)

☐ **FRANKIE AND JOHNNY IN THE CLAIR DE LUNE by Terrence McNally.** Charged with racy humor and searing intimacy, this unforgettable play offers a dramatic vision of sexuality, commitment, and love in modern life that strikes unsparingly, inescapably home.   (268842—$6.95)

☐ **PRELUDE TO A KISS by Craig Lucas.** An award-winning play that transforms a classic romantic fairy tale into a stunningly powerful evocation of sex, death, and compassion in times that are far from compassionate. "Enchanting, charming, mysterious . . . Craig Lucas is a born playwright!"—*The New Yorker*   (265673—$8.00)

Prices slightly higher in Canada.

Buy them at your local bookstore or use this convenient coupon for ordering.

PENGUIN USA
P.O. Box 999, Dept. #17109
Bergenfield, New Jersey 07621

Please send me the books I have checked above.
I am enclosing $_____ (please add $2.00 to cover postage and handling).
Send check or money order (no cash or C.O.D.'s) or charge by Mastercard or VISA (with a $15.00 minimum). Prices and numbers are subject to change without notice.

Card # _____ Exp. Date _____
Signature _____
Name _____
Address _____
City _____ State _____ Zip Code _____

For faster service when ordering by credit card call **1-800-253-6476**

Allow a minimum of 4-6 weeks for delivery. This offer is subject to change without notice